KU-645-709

MORE BOOKS BY ADAM CROFT

RUTLAND CRIME SERIES

1. What Lies Beneath
2. On Borrowed Time
3. In Cold Blood

KNIGHT & CULVERHOUSE CRIME THRILLERS

1. Too Close for Comfort
2. Guilty as Sin
3. Jack Be Nimble
4. Rough Justice
5. In Too Deep
6. In The Name of the Father
7. With A Vengeance
8. Dead & Buried
9. In Plain Sight
10. Snakes & Ladders

PSYCHOLOGICAL THRILLERS

- Her Last Tomorrow
- Only The Truth

ON BORROWED TIME

ADAM CROFT

BLACK CANNON
PUBLISHING

First published in Great Britain in 2020.

This edition published in 2021 by Black Cannon Publishing.

ISBN: 978-1-912599-54-7

Copyright © Adam Croft 2020

The right of Adam Croft to be identified as the author of this work has been asserted by him in accordance with the Copyright, Designs and Patents Act 1988.

All rights reserved. No part of this book may be reproduced in any form or by any electronic or mechanical means, including information storage and retrieval systems, without written permission from the author, except for the use of brief quotations in a book review.

This is a work of fiction. Names, characters, businesses, places, events, locales, and incidents are either the products of the author's imagination or used in a fictitious manner. Any resemblance to actual persons, living or dead, or actual events is purely coincidental.

A CIP catalogue record for this book is available from the British Library.

Printed and bound in Great Britain by Clays Ltd, Elcograf S.p.A.

- In Her Image
- Tell Me I'm Wrong
- The Perfect Lie
- Closer To You

KEMPSTON HARDWICK MYSTERIES

1. Exit Stage Left
2. The Westerlea House Mystery
3. Death Under the Sun
4. The Thirteenth Room
5. The Wrong Man

All titles are available to order from all good book shops.

Signed and personalised editions available at adamcroft.net/shop.

Foreign language editions of some titles are available in French, German, Italian, Portuguese, Dutch and Korean. These are available online and in book shops in their native countries.

EBOOK-ONLY SHORT STORIES

- Gone
- The Harder They Fall
- Love You To Death
- The Defender

To find out more, visit adamcroft.net

HAVE YOU LISTENED TO THE
RUTLAND AUDIOBOOKS?

The Rutland crime series is now available in audiobook format, narrated by Leicester-born **Andy Nyman** (Peaky Blinders, Unforgotten, Star Wars).

They are available from all good audiobook retailers and libraries now, published by W.F. Howes on their QUEST and Clipper imprints.

W.F. Howes are one of the world's largest audiobook publishers and have been based in Leicestershire since their inception.

W.F. HOWES LTD
QUEST

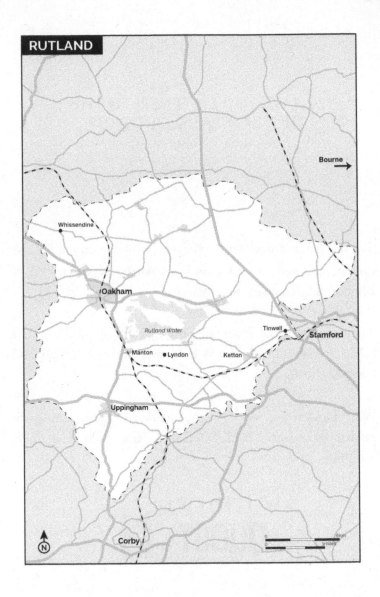

RUTLAND

Bourne →

Whissendine

Oakham

Rutland Water

Tinwell

Stamford

Manton ● Lyndon

Ketton

Uppingham

Corby

N

0   6km
0   3miles

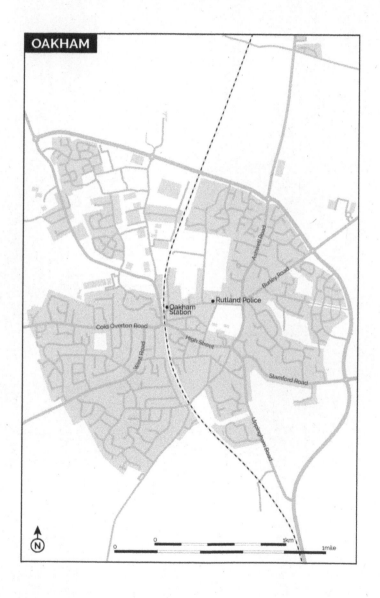

OAKHAM

Anwell Road
Burley Road
Rutland Police
Oakham Station
Cold Overton Road
West Road
High Street
Stamford Road
Uppingham Road

N

0
0
1km
1mile

1

Gary Stoddart quite liked the early shift. It meant departing
Nottingham at four minutes to five in the morning, but would
see him home not long after lunch. Besides, what could be
better than watching the sun rise as he drove his train through
the beautiful East Midlands countryside?

He watched a small number of early-morning commuters
boarding the carriages as the 5.49am service came to a brief
rest in Oakham, before it would set off again, along the South
Shore of Rutland Water and on to Stamford.

There'd been a stunning mist sitting on the fields between
Melton Mowbray and Oakham — something which'd probably have cleared within the hour, and which drivers working
later turns wouldn't get to admire. There was always something about crisp early mornings that excited him. And this
early morning was as-yet unbroken. Although this was the first
eastbound service of the day, there'd usually been at least two
earlier westbound trains by now — not to mention a slew of
overnight freight. But nighttime engineering works further

along the line meant Gary's train was the first of the day, breaking through the virgin mist of the Rutland countryside.

With his new set of passengers on board, Gary pulled away from Oakham Station, pleased to see he hadn't caused too much frustration on the level crossing in the centre of town, and started to gather speed as the train headed south.

This was his favourite part of the run. Once the train was clear of Oakham it'd follow the A6003 and enter the tunnel which ran under the village of Manton, before the track split and headed east between Rutland Water and the A47, then dipped under the Great North Road and into the picturesque market town of Stamford.

He'd always found it rather odd that the train line went directly underneath Manton, when it could just as easily have gone round it. Then again, he only drove the things; he hadn't built the line.

The overnight engineering works meant speed restrictions had been put in place on this stretch. Gary didn't mind, even if his passengers did. The joy of driving a train wasn't connected with speed. And in any case, it gave him more time to enjoy his surroundings — something he knew he'd never grow tired of.

The train gathered speed, piercing through the mist as it began to soar over the A6003, the entrance to the Manton tunnel opening up ahead. As it did, Gary noticed something that caught his eye. His instincts kicking in, he cut the throttle and hit the brakes, praying he'd spotted it early enough.

The morning had been damp, and the friction wasn't kicking in anywhere near as quickly as Gary would've liked, despite the speed restrictions that were in place. In a split-second, he made the decision to slam on the emergency brakes, adrenaline pumping in his chest and his stomach lurching as he realised what was about to happen.

He did exactly what he'd been trained not to do, and closed his eyes. He waited for the inevitable, sickening noise as the train screeched to a halt, jolting him in his seat.

Silence. A brief moment where he wondered if he'd dreamt the whole thing.

Slowly, Gary opened his eyes and looked out through the windscreen of his cab.

It was the detail that struck him first. The fabric. The gentle sway. The milky whites of the eyes. It was only a second or two later that his mind registered the dead body hanging just inches away from him.

Caroline Hills groaned as she felt the cold porcelain against her chest. It had become a familiar sensation, along with seeing the slight chip on the inside of the rim, where she'd dropped a slate toothbrush holder on the day they'd moved into the house.

It would be fair to say there were quite a few downsides to dealing with cancer, and making friends with the toilet bowl was certainly one of them. Her original treatment had been relatively easy to deal with, but it hadn't been altogether successful. As a result, the doctors had taken the decision to step it up a gear, and it'd hit Caroline hard.

'Are you okay?' her husband, Mark, mumbled through the door of their en-suite bathroom.

'I'm fine. You go back to bed.'

Although she felt exhausted, there was no way she'd be able to get back to sleep. Once she was up, she was up. Even if it was only half six in the morning. Mark, on the other hand, could steal an extra hour or two's kip. It'd do him good. He'd had to take up the slack when Caroline had been unable to be at her best, and had supported her through every step. At least, he had once he'd actually known about it.

Caroline had made the decision shortly after being diagnosed with ovarian cancer to deal with it herself. Mark had only recently lost his own brother and father to cancer, and the family had been through more than enough. It was something she believed she could fight on her own, but she'd been proven wrong.

Fighting battles alone was something she was used to. The irony wasn't lost on her that her private life was so different from her work, in which she was used to being part of a team, sharing information and collaborating for the greater good as a Detective Inspector with Rutland Police. When it came to her private life, things were different.

She and Mark had always been close, but there were aspects of her past even he didn't know about. She hadn't kept them from him for any other reason than to protect him and keep the peace, but even so, the growing feeling of guilt was starting to gnaw away at her. She often wondered if the reason why she and Mark were so close was that they didn't need to rely on each other for emotional support. Until Mark's dad and brother died, they'd had no major tragedies to deal with. There'd been ups and downs, of course, but never anything big and never anything which had needed a heart-to-heart. Their deaths had hit Mark hard, and Caroline hadn't wanted to burden him any further.

She'd always been good at keeping her work close to her chest. When they'd lived in London and she'd worked for the Met, it had been drummed into her to not divulge details of cases she was working on. More often than not, those cases involved powerful gangs and underground criminal networks. In Rutland, that was rarely the case. Indeed, in Rutland it was almost impossible to keep anything confidential. She sometimes wondered if the locals should be briefing her on what had happened. It was a different way of working; a different pace of life. But it was one she was starting to respect and enjoy.

She certainly wouldn't have wanted to be dealing with cancer and chemotherapy whilst living in Cricklewood. Here, the peace and quiet, the scenery – and, yes, the people – were selflessly and unknowingly providing ample comfort and support. Trips to Peterborough City Hospital were just part of the package.

The last wave of nausea disappeared at the same time she registered the sound of her mobile phone vibrating on her beside table. She flushed the toilet, opened the door and walked over to answer it. She could see from the name on the screen it was Dexter Antoine, a Detective Sergeant on her team.

'Morning, Dex. I'm guessing this isn't a polite wake-up call?'

'Nope. Fix up, look sharp. We've got a body.'

'Dex, it's Monday morning. Listen, you've got good community relations round here. Can you tell people to stop dying so early in the morning please?'

'I'll do my best, but we might be a bit late for this chap. On the plus side, it's been called in as a suicide, so you might still be home for brunch.'

'Little mercies, eh? And why am I being called out to deal with a suicide?'

'Ah yeah, I forgot there was a word before "suicide".'

'Which was?'

'"Suspicious."'

'Wonderful. Who decided that?'

'First responders. One of them reckoned there're a couple of things that don't look right. I'm on my way down there now. Apparently they tried to get hold of you, but there was no answer. I told them you'd probably had a heavy night.'

'Oh great, thanks Dex.'

'Pleasure!'

'So where am I going?' she said, opening her wardrobe and pulling out some clothes.

'Do you know Manton?'

'Loosely. I know where it is.'

'Right. When you get there, you want to head down Cemetery Lane.'

'Cemetery Lane? Is this some sort of joke?'

'Well, no. There's a cemetery on it.'

'And that's where the body is?'

'Nope. That's where I'll meet you. Bring a decent pair of shoes, won't you?'

A little over fifteen minutes later, Caroline parked her Volvo in a bay outside the Horse and Jockey pub in Manton.

She vaguely recognised it as being on one of Mark's favourite cycle routes, and noticed the bike racks outside, ready to welcome the day's cyclists when the pub opened later that day. Dexter was sitting propped against a low wall at the side of the Horse and Jockey, his hands in his pockets. He nodded as she approached him.

'Morning. Find it alright?'

'Sat nav,' Caroline replied, holding up her phone.

'Where we're going, we won't need a sat nav.'

'Never had you down as a Back to the Future fan, Dex.'

'No, I mean literally. You heard what I said about the shoes, right?'

Caroline followed Dexter down Cemetery Lane – a narrow, winding track to the side of the Horse and Jockey. Before long, the promised cemetery appeared on their left, before another track spurred off to their right.

'Up here,' Dexter said. 'It doglegs back on itself a bit as it goes uphill. Hope your calf muscles are warmed up.'

Dexter strode up the cycle path with Caroline in tow. After a few seconds, she noticed the train line down below, with some clear activity happening in the mouth of the tunnel.

'Dex, stop. I'm having trouble holding onto my stomach this morning as it is. Tell me now: have we got a jumper?'

'Nope. A dangler.'

'In the tunnel?'

'Sort of. In the mouth of it. The tunnel runs right underneath Manton and comes out the other side. The whole village is built over the train line. Our customer was found hanging in the mouth of the tunnel.'

'Christ. Who found him?' she said, marching after Dexter again.

'Train driver.'

'Dex, stop again.'

'No need. He hit the brakes. Your stomach's fine.'

AT THE TOP of the hill, the path turned to cross the railway, then banked back down along the far side of the track, in the direction from which they'd just come, but east of the railway.

'Where does that go?' Caroline asked.

'Joins the A6003 by the bridge. Popular cycle route, apparently.'

'Not today, it won't be.' She looked down at the path,

noticing what looked like fresh tyre marks in the dirt. 'Look at that, Dex. Looks recent.'

'Yeah. I know. I was hoping you weren't going to say that.'

Caroline said her hellos to the officers at the scene and took in everything in front of her. From her position, she could see along the railway line in the direction of Oakham as it ran right under her feet. Behind her, the village of Manton. From here, she couldn't see the mouth of the tunnel, but she could easily see how someone could access it. A small fence separated the path from a bank of scrubland, which sloped down towards the mouth of the tunnel, with only a cursory metal barrier at the edge.

'Has someone been down here?' Caroline asked, gesturing to the trodden-down foliage on the bank.

'Yeah, it's the only way to get access. But I know what you're thinking, and yes, it was fairly well trodden when we arrived,' PC Joe Lloyd said. 'That's what made us think it wasn't quite right. Looks to me like someone's dragged him down from here, then tied him to the metal barrier and lobbed him off.'

'It's possible,' Caroline said, crossing her fingers and hoping that wouldn't turn out to be the case. 'I'll need a list of everyone who's been down there for elimination purposes. We'll need SOCO to comb it all for fibres. There's no way someone's got down there and back without leaving a trace. It looks brutal.'

'Nettles, brambles, the lot,' PC Lloyd said. 'Wouldn't fancy my chances without a decent pair of boots and some waders. We can get to it round the side now, if you like. They've closed the line.'

Caroline and Dexter followed PC Lloyd further along the track as it snaked back down on the far side of the railway line. As they reached the bottom of the hill, she noticed someone had already rigged up a set of steps for getting over the low fence and onto the train line. She looked to her right, at the diesel locomotive stopped on the track, having been reversed back from the tunnel entrance.

'Where's the driver?' she asked.

'Having a sit down behind the train. He didn't fancy seeing the body again, funnily enough.'

'So what happened?' Caroline asked as they approached the mouth of the tunnel.

'Our boy the driver, Gary Stoddart, he's left Oakham station and is on his way to Stamford. He says there was a speed restriction in place because of engineering works, and that's the only reason he'd managed to stop in time. Otherwise, it'd be a proper messy job,' PC Lloyd said.

'What time was this?'

'A few minutes before six. The train left Oakham around five-fifty. Probably takes a minute or two to get here. Maybe a bit more with speed restrictions.'

'And when was the last train to come through here before that?'

'Yeah, we thought of that. The lad was hanging right in the middle of the tunnel, so he'd have been hit by any train coming in either direction. There was overnight engineering works, though. This train was the first one of the day.'

Caroline looked at the body in front of her. She didn't like to make too many assumptions without evidence, but some things were clear. It was a male, late twenties or early thirties, and he hadn't been strung up in the few minutes before he was found. She could see from the colour of his skin that he'd been dead at least a couple of hours.

'Where were the engineering works?' she asked.

'Just south of Manton Junction.'

'Can't see them from here?'

'Nope. Probably wouldn't hear them, either.'

Caroline slowly nodded. Whether he'd hanged himself or someone else had put him there, one thing seemed clear: the intention had been for him to be hit by an earlier train, ensuring certain death and making identification of the body a lot more difficult.

'Any ID?' Caroline asked.

'Nothing. Just the clothes he's wearing.'

'What state were they in?'

'Fine. That's the weird thing about it. If he'd been dragged down there, his clothes'd be in a right state. Something's clearly been dragged down, though. You can tell by the state of the ground.'

'But not him, perhaps. It looks like there're some tyre tracks round the bend there.'

'Yeah, I noticed those. They were there before we got here. The only way in's the way you just came,' PC Lloyd said. 'There's a gate and bollards down the other end. Just about wide enough for a bike or two, but there's no way you'd get a car in. Or out.'

'Difficult to turn around, though.'

'I wouldn't fancy it. But if you've got a small enough car, I reckon it'd be doable up the top there. Probably more of a twenty-seven-point turn than a three-point-turn, but it's not like anyone's watching. It's either that or reverse all the way back out, and that wouldn't be any easier.'

'Has anyone spoken to that pub on the corner? Horse and Jockey, was it?'

'Not yet.'

'Alright. Can you, please? We'll need to get hold of their external CCTV. With any luck, there'll be a camera pointing the right way and we'll be able to identify any vehicles that came down this track. Am I right in thinking they'd have to drive past the pub?'

'Yeah, I can't see how they'd manage it otherwise.'

'Alright, good. Excellent. That's got to be our best shot, then.'

'If the cameras are working,' PC Lloyd said, causing Caroline's heart to sink.

'Yeah. If the cameras are working.'

Caroline nodded and smiled at the pathologist, Dr David Duncan, who she vaguely recognised. She had no idea how he'd managed to get here before her, especially as he lived further afield, but she looked on agog as he stood a little way away from the body, jotting down notes with one hand whilst popping Hula Hoops in his mouth with the other. Caroline walked over to him, noticing a few crumbs stuck in his greying beard as she greeted him.

Dr Duncan spoke with a velvety baritone voice which wouldn't have sounded out of place on a luxury chocolate ad. 'I must say, DI Hills, you're very good for business. It used to be a rare treat to come out to Rutland, but I can almost set my watch by the murder rate since you've arrived.'

'Alright, thank you. I don't need reminding. Is it murder then?'

'Ah, now you know jolly well that's not for me to say. But if I were you I wouldn't be taking any holidays any time soon. There's some bruising and chafing around the neck which isn't entirely consistent with hanging. You can see where it's tugged and bruised the skin. I'd say he's been pulled down here.'

'Dead or alive?'

'Tricky to say. Not dead long, if he was. Either killed just before he was dragged down, or heavily sedated. There's no sign of incongruous lividity. If he'd been dead for a little while before being hanged, I'd expect to see the blood pooling at its lowest point. Here, that's the feet. So he was either killed shortly before being dragged down here, or he was brought in bolt upright on a roof rack.'

Caroline couldn't help but chuckle at the imagery. Gallows humour was often a required ingredient of the job. 'Could he have been alive when he was brought down?'

'Possible. If he was alive, he was sedated, because there are no signs he tried to remove the noose. We'll have to do a toxicology report to confirm.'

'Smells like he'd been drinking pretty heavily. Would that do the trick?'

'Unlikely. Although he might've drunk himself into a deep sleep and not been able to react quickly enough to strangulation, for example. Especially if it was forceful enough to damage the windpipe or just happened to catch the vagus nerve. If you apply enough pressure to just the right point on the side of the neck here, it causes a rapid drop in heart rate and blood pressure and can easily render someone uncon-scious. If your man here had low blood pressure anyway, that effect could be achieved more easily. Alcohol would've reduced his blood pressure, too. It's entirely possible he might've had a head start. We'll be able to confirm in more detail once we've got him on the slab, but there's certainly some odd bruising which could well be consistent with prior strangulation. I wouldn't like to say just yet, though.'

Caroline looked back at the body — the third since she'd arrived in Rutland — and mentally prepared herself for what was to come.

4

As if a murder case on a Monday morning wasn't enough for
Caroline, she arrived at work to a note on her desk asking her
to head to Chief Superintendent Derek Arnold's office.
Arnold point-blank refused to phone or email anyone in the
same building, and was frequently seen roaming the corridors
in search of whoever he was looking for. Caroline, on the other
hand, preferred a bit of space and thinking time — something
that wasn't possible when under the pressure of an unnecessary face-to-face meeting.

Arnold's way of doing things meant she had no idea what
he wanted to talk about until she was seated at his desk — by
which time it was too late. It was something else which made
him appear daunting and formidable, although Caroline was
starting to see something else under that exterior.

She knocked on the door of his office and waited to be
called in.

'Ah, morning. I won't keep you long,' he said. 'I hear

you've got a bit of a job on your hands. How's it all shaping up?'

'Very early days, but we're making fast progress. I think once we've got an ID we'll be a lot closer.'

'Is there still a possibility it wasn't murder at all?'

'Well, yes. Sort of. There are fresh tyre tracks. I suppose they could've been there longer, but you'd expect them to be gone by then due to the amount of foot and bike traffic that path gets. Besides which, we've had rain over the past few days, so I'd expect them to have been washed away if they were any more than a day or so old. He obviously didn't drive himself up and then drive his own car away.'

'Fingers crossed there's another answer. Last thing we want is another murder on our doorstep. That won't do the crime figures any good at all.'

Nor the families of those who've lost loved ones, Caroline wanted to say, but didn't.

'But anyway,' he said, changing the subject. 'How are you getting on otherwise? With the... you know.'

'Cancer.'

'Yeah, that.'

'It'll be a long haul, but I'm doing alright.'

'I've noticed the... you know.'

'The hat.'

'Yes.'

'I've been getting some hair loss. Bit of a temporary measure, really.'

'I see. And do you think you'll be getting a... you know.'

'A wig.'

'Yes. One of those.'

'I don't know. Maybe. Part of me wants to cling on to what I've got and carry on as normal, and the other half wants to say "sod the lot of you", shave it all off and stick a finger up at anyone who takes a second glance.'

'Well, there are probably other ways of fostering better community relations, but I see your point. And what about energy levels and things? How are you coping?'

'Fine.'

'Because I was thinking, if this does turn out to be a murder case after all, it might be an idea to pass it on to EMSOU. Purely because of the timing, I mean. The last thing I'd want is to create unnecessary pressure for you.'

'It's not unnecessary. It's literally my job.'

With Rutland Police being the smallest force in the country — by quite some way — it was usual for major crimes to be handed to the East Midlands Special Operations Unit. Caroline, though, being an experienced detective who'd worked for the Metropolitan Police in London, had other ideas.

Arnold shuffled in his chair. 'I mean, by rights we should be handing it over anyway. It's highly irregular for Rutland to be taking on its own murder cases.'

'It's highly irregular for Rutland to have murder cases full-stop. But I've got the experience and the track record.'

'Yes, well I think it's probably best we don't talk about track records. You know how intensely uncomfortable Operation Forelock was.'

'I certainly do.'

'Which is why I think it might be best to at least provide you with some additional support from EMSOU. That's not

to say you can't be involved. I just think it would be a derelic-
tion of my duty as your superior if I let you take this on alone,
considering the circumstances.'

'I told you the circumstances. I feel fine. With respect, you
don't get to decide how I feel or what I'm capable of.'

Arnold sighed. 'Listen, there's no need to overreact. If
we're still investigating the suicide angle and there's a good
chance this chap killed himself, it doesn't need to be an issue
at all. You know, maybe it would be best if it did turn out to be
a suicide after all.'

'Even if it isn't, it still doesn't need to be an issue. You're
the only one who seems to want to turn it into one.'

'I just want what's best for you and the rest of the team,
Caroline.'

Caroline stood up. 'Good. In that case, I'll get back to
work.'

5

Back in the incident room, Caroline prepared to brief her small but able team. There seemed to be less energy and enthusiasm than she'd expected, almost as if they were antici-pating her announcing the case would be handed over to EMSOU. But she hoped what she was about to say would focus a few minds.

'Right. First of all, thank you for all the work you've been doing so far on this already. The computer kindly tells us we should be referring to it as Operation Utopia. And yes, that means we're keeping hold of the case.' She could tell from looking at the faces of Dexter Antoine, Sara Henshaw and Aidan Chilcott that there was an undercurrent of unease. 'Does anyone have any questions at this point?'

Aidan raised his hand. 'Is it a good idea, so soon after Operation Forelock?'

'What's the timing got to do with anything?' Caroline asked. 'I'm not being funny, but we managed to close that case, and this one looks like child's play in comparison.'

'But it nearly went so wrong.'

'Nearly. But it didn't, did it?' She wouldn't admit to her team that she had, of course, had reservations of her own. Not only had she been taken off Operation Forelock and had the case handed over to EMSOU, but she'd come face to face with the killer they'd been hunting after she made an eleventh-hour discovery that had revealed his identity. She swallowed hard as the flashbacks hit her and she recalled how close she'd come to being his final victim. 'In any case, we don't have time to worry about daft procedural issues. They're for me to deal with. Let's crack on. Sara, we've managed to get ID on the body?'

'We have. He's Thomas Medland, known to friends and family as Tom. Thirty-four years old, from Barleythorpe. Lived locally all his life. He was married for a while but was recently divorced and living back with his parents. They reported him missing this morning when he hadn't come home from the pub last night.'

'Pub? Where was he drinking?'

'All over Oakham, apparently. I think he's well-known in a few local places. Well-liked too, apparently. Didn't get much more than that. Figured we should probably save it for a sit-down chat. We've got an FLO with them.'

Caroline nodded. Family Liaison Officers were specially trained to deal with bereaved families and the victims of crime. 'Okay, thanks Sara. Anything else from forensics or pathology at the moment?'

'Not yet. He stank of alcohol, apparently, which isn't surprising if he'd been at the pub. Didn't seem to be any injuries on the body other than what we'd expect from a hanging. We're still waiting on an official report, though.'

'Alright. Good. Let's get his photo circulated around the pubs, see where he was last night. From there, let's follow as far as we can on CCTV. See who he talked to, who he left with, where he went. Did he get into any fights or altercations? Ask the publicans, ask the locals. Let's get on top of this from the off. Get onto the phone network and find out where Tom's mobile went, too. He's unlikely to have gone out without it, so we can trace his movements using cell site data and work our way back from there. Dexter, we'll go and speak to the parents and see what we can get from them. Everyone clear on what they're doing?' She watched as her team nodded, now seemingly more fired up than they had been a few moments ago, and felt a fire within her own belly.

6

Caroline drove out to Barleythorpe, formerly a village in its own right, but having more recently become the de facto north-west conurbation of Oakham. As they approached Tom Medland's parents' house, Derek Arnold's words rang in Caroline's ears.

Maybe it would be best if it did turn out to be a suicide after all.

She couldn't help but read between the lines — even if they didn't exist. Was he suggesting that she should try to write Tom Medland's death off as suicide, regardless of her suspicions to the contrary? Proving murder might well turn out to be difficult in itself, never mind identifying a killer. But what if her suspicions turned out to bear fruit? She couldn't, in all conscience, bring herself to sweep anything under the carpet to save Arnold's precious statistics and crime figures. As far as she was concerned, justice had to be done — at all costs. It was the only way the circle of life could continue unpolluted.

They pulled up outside the house of Jerry and Lorraine Medland, and Caroline switched off the engine.

'Nice enough place,' Dexter said.

'If there's one thing I've learned over the years, it's that the amount of money and size of house you've got means absolutely nothing when it comes to things like this. Murder transcends social boundaries. And when it doesn't, it's usually money that's caused it in the first place.'

The Family Liaison Officer was already waiting for them when they arrived, disappearing into the kitchen to make cups of tea and leaving them to speak to Jerry and Lorraine in peace.

'First of all, can I say how sorry we are for your loss,' Caroline said, affecting a reaction in Lorraine Medland which sounded like it was the first time she'd heard the news.

'Sorry,' Jerry said, comforting his wife. 'It's just it hits us every now and again. Doesn't quite sink in, you know? Your brain sort of adjusts for a minute or two, then — wallop — there it is.'

Tom's parents were older than Caroline had imagined them to be. If Tom was thirty-four, she'd expected Jerry and Lorraine to be somewhere around sixty, but she estimated they were a good ten years older than that.

'I understand you've already been told what happened?'

Jerry nodded. 'Yes. But it doesn't make any sense. There's no way Tom did that to himself. He wouldn't. He had no reason to.'

'He was divorced, wasn't he?' Dexter asked.

In an instant, Jerry's face turned sour. 'We'll not talk about that. But you can take it from me, Tom never let things like that get to him. He used to pick himself up and get on with it. Always happy, always chipper. There's no way he would've done a thing like that.'

Tom's mum started wailing again at the thought, and Caroline felt a stab of pain in her own chest. The thought of losing a child was unbearable, and at times like this she had to separate her own motherhood from the job in hand. If she let her thoughts run away with her, she'd never be able to do anything.

'Does his wife still live locally?' Caroline asked.

Jerry shook his head. 'Buggered off back to China.'

'She was Chinese?'

'As they come. She was only over here for university. Tom met her on a night out in Leicester. Weaselled her way in, got married, then lost interest and decided she didn't fancy the green card after all, and jumped on the first plane home.'

'Has she been back since?'

'Not bloody likely. Haven't heard hide nor hair of her since.'

Dexter took down the wife's details, and made a note to check with the border authorities that there was no record of her being back in the UK. They'd have to track her down and speak to her as a matter of course, but that would be a matter for Interpol.

'Do you know who Tom was out with last night? We understand he was at the pub. Do you know which one? Or if he'd arranged to meet anyone?'

Again, Jerry Medland failed to hide the disdain on his face. 'I don't know, but I've got my suspicions.'

'Go on.'

'His cousin, Charlie. Charlie Ford. The lad's an absolute scumbag, if you ask me.'

The name rang a vague bell in Caroline's mind, but she wasn't sure why. 'What makes you say that?' she asked.

'Check your computers when you get back to the nick and see for yourself. Off the top of my head: burglary, car theft, shoplifting and assault.'

'He's got a record?'

'Record? He's got more records than Woolworths. And if you ask me, I reckon he's moved into drugs. Always flashing the cash about, driving new cars, swanning off on holiday. You don't manage that on a bit of burglary and nicking the odd tea towel from Wilko's.'

'And did Tom hang around with him regularly?'

'Too regularly for my liking. Charlie came round here yesterday looking for him, but I sent him away. Wouldn't surprise me one bit if they met up later. Not much I can do about it, though, is there? Tom's a grown man. Was.'

Caroline watched as the act of correcting his son's existence into the past tense almost sent Jerry over the edge. 'I'm sorry to have to ask you this, but was Tom ever involved in any crime? Do you think he might have been into drugs in some way?'

'He wouldn't do crime. No. He was the sort of lad who liked to live and let live. He wouldn't have a go at Charlie for it, but there was no way he'd do it himself.'

'And drugs?'

'Well, you never know, do you? I wouldn't have said he was that sort of lad, but how can you ever know what's going on inside someone else's head?'

Caroline had to agree. She shared a look with Dexter, the unspoken possibilities passing through both their minds. Had Tom been involved with the drugs scene? It was an unfortunate truth that drugs debts often led to violence. A man who was recently divorced and forced to live with his parents would be a prime candidate for falling into that trap. Or had drugs contributed to a spiralling depression, causing him to take his own life? Either way, what had initially seemed to be a fairly straightforward case was now deepening and getting more sinister by the minute.

7

Jerry Medland had told Caroline and Dexter that Charlie Ford lived on a farm just outside Tinwell. He'd been keen to point out that Charlie only rented an outbuilding, and that any delusions of grandeur on his part should be taken with a rather large pinch of salt.

As they made their way over, Aidan called to say Tom's mobile phone appeared to have been switched off since late last night, and that the phone network were sending over the data, which could be used to triangulate his location the previous evening.

When they arrived at the farm, they were surprised to see how run-down the place looked. It wasn't immediately clear whether it was still a working farm, and it seemed to Caroline as if something else might be going on under the surface.

They parked up in the gravel yard next to a shipping container, and Caroline looked around at the scene in front of her. There was a rusty, mouldy old caravan in one corner of the yard, as well as what looked to her like some sort of empty cattle shed. The main farm house was separated from this area by a high wall, having been sold off some years earlier. Charlie's outbuilding was a little further down, almost masked by a yew hedge which, at first, made it invisible from the main yard.

They walked up to the building and knocked on the door, wondering if perhaps they should have brought a larger team with them. It wasn't unusual for people living on farms round here to own guns, but Caroline doubted whether Charlie Ford would ever be granted a firearms licence with his track record. A short while later, the door opened.

The man who answered simply stood and looked at them, as if waiting for them to speak first.

'Hello. Charlie Ford?' Caroline asked.

'What about him?'

'Are you Charlie?'

'Depends who's asking.'

'Are you the sort of person who usually changes his identity based on who's asking?'

'Coppers, then.'

'Detective Inspector Caroline Hills and Detective Sergeant Dexter Antoine. Your turn.'

'What's this about?' the man said, leaning against the wooden doorframe and folding his arms.

'It's about your cousin, Tom Medland.'

'Yeah, well you're too late. My mum already phoned and told me.'

'Oh we're not here to break the news,' Dexter said. 'We're here to ask you a few questions.'

Charlie looked at Dexter as if he'd just fallen out the back of a refuse truck. 'Such as?'

'Such as when you last saw Tom,' Caroline said.

'He was alive when I last saw him, so that won't be much use to you. Now, if you don't mind I've got some paint I need to watch drying.'

'I do mind actually, yes. We need to trace his last movements and hoped you might be able to help us.'

Charlie laughed. 'Help you? Get lost. I don't owe you nothing. You lot have done me over enough times over the years, you can piss off if you think I'm helping you now.'

'Charlie, we have good reason to believe Tom was murdered.' Caroline could see from the look on his face that this had come as a shock to Charlie.

'What?'

'When did you last see Tom?'

Charlie seemed to think about this for a moment. 'We had a few drinks yesterday.'

'Where? When?'

Charlie sighed. 'All over. Grainstore. Railway. Wheatsheaf. Usual circuit.'

'In Oakham?'

'Yeah. We fancied doing a bit of a crawl, so only really got Stamford or Oakham. I've got to get a cab wherever we go, so we figured we'd make it easier on Tom.'

'And what happened at the end of the night? How did you get home?'

'Like I said, a cab.'

'With Tom?'

'Nah, he walked back. I offered him to jump in with me, but he said he wanted the walk.'

'And was that the last you heard from him?'

'Yeah. I hit the sack when I got in. His phone ran out of battery while we was in the pub, so I wasn't exactly waiting for a text or anything.'

'What time did his phone die?'

'Dunno. Not long before we went back, to be honest. Left about ten, so his phone probably died about half-nine.'

'Which way did he walk?'

Charlie looked at Caroline as if she'd just dropped out of the sky. 'Towards home, obviously.'

'And in a little more detail?'

Charlie sighed petulantly. 'We left the Wheatsheaf, he turned left down Northgate. Presumably crossed the railway line and up Barleythorpe Road. Couldn't you've worked that one out yourself?'

Caroline ignored the barb. 'And was it just alcohol you'd been taking?' she asked.

Charlie looked her dead in the eye. 'Yes. You don't want to listen to what my Uncle Jerry says. And yeah, I know you'll have got that from him. He caught me with one spliff behind my mum's garage when I was fifteen, and now he thinks I'm Pablo bloody Escobar.'

'So to confirm, neither you nor Tom had taken any other substances?' Dexter asked.

'I had a Nurofen yesterday lunchtime if that counts. Twisted my knee a couple of weeks back and didn't want it swelling up while we was walking round.'

Caroline forced a smile. 'Which cab company did you use?'

'Berridge's.'

Caroline saw Dexter jot that down in his notebook to follow up later on.

'And did they take you straight home?'

'Yeah, obviously.'

'Were you here all night?'

'Well, yeah. Not exactly a hub of nightlife round here, you know what I mean?'

'Any alibi?'

'There's a couple of goats somewhere over there who might've peeped through the gap in the curtains, but that's about the best I can do. Anyway, I know what your game is. You've been over to speak to Uncle Jerry, he's told you I'm a wrong'un, whaddya know I'm the last person to see Tom alive, and I daresay you've already found out I'm on your books with previous. Don't worry, I would've come to the same conclusion if I was in your shoes.'

'And what conclusion's that?' Caroline asked innocently.

'You lot thinking I had something to do with Tom's death. But I'm telling you now, you're barking up the wrong tree.'

8

The first twenty-four hours of any investigation were crucial, and Caroline felt they'd made decent progress already as she held the team's Monday afternoon briefing.

'Alright, so there's a lot we already know, and a lot we're still waiting for. Our biggest bet has to be CCTV from the Horse and Jockey pub. I had a look on my way out earlier and there are cameras pointing at the parking spaces across the lane, so they'll have picked up any cars going in or out. And we know our man must have either gone in or out that way. There's no other option. It's an old CCTV system, and they're still wrestling with it, but the good news is that apparently it does work. It's looked after by a security company, though, and getting hold of them is proving problematic. Dex, we had news from the SOCOs, didn't we?'

'Sort of, yeah. They reckoned there's some indication that Tom might've been strangled before the rope was tied round his neck. They can't be certain at the moment, but should have something a bit more definite before too long. Obviously, that'd be the point of no return because then we'd know we're definitely looking for a killer.'

'Toxicology timeframe?'

'A while yet. We're trying to pull some strings, but I think we might have a wait on our hands.'

'Okay. Time-wise, we could be looking at anything from half ten last night to a few minutes before six this morning. Engineering works at Manton Junction meant there were no trains running between those times. He wasn't there when the last train yesterday went through the tunnel, but was when the first train did today. Sara, Aidan, did we get anything from the pubs Tom went into in Oakham?'

'No, nothing of any real note,' Sara said. 'We know he went into the Grainstore at around quarter past six, and Charlie arrived a few minutes later. They stayed there for two pints, then went to the Railway just before seven. They left there at about eight and went to the Wheatsheaf, where they stayed until closing time, which is ten o'clock on Sundays.'

'And Tom's phone?'

'Goes off in the Wheatsheaf at nine-forty.'

'Which is when Charlie said Tom's battery went. It also means it's unlikely he got to Manton before the Horse and Jockey closed for the night. What we need to find out is how he got there. Did he leave the Wheatsheaf on foot?'

'Yep. They both waited until Charlie's cab turned up to take him back home. Then CCTV shows Tom turning left and heading down Northgate, presumably to cross over the train line and head home. CCTV at the station never picks him up, though. We have no idea how he got from Northgate to Manton.'

'Right. Okay,' Caroline said. 'I'm still confident the footage from the Horse and Jockey will be the key here. If we can identify a car on that, we can trace the owner. Either that or we can cross-reference that with CCTV from Oakham. There's a decent chance Tom was picked up in town and taken to Manton by his killer. If we're pretty certain he didn't cross the railway, I think that's got to be our strongest lead. In the meantime, let's keep knocking on doors. Family, friends, colleagues. Get as much information as we can, so when that footage comes in we've got the strongest case possible.'

Caroline watched as her team nodded. 'What about his ex-wife? Have we managed to track her down yet?' she asked.

'She's been informed,' Sara said. 'She's not left China since she arrived back from the UK after the divorce, and there's no indication she had any reason to want Tom dead. She didn't even want any money from their divorce. Sounds like she just wanted to put the whole thing behind her.'

'Right,' Caroline said, sighing. 'Then it looks like we've got some work to do.'

9

The low evening light streamed in through the large window in the Lord Nelson as the sun started to set. Sophie Lawson dipped her head slightly to avoid being dazzled, and took a sip of her gin and tonic. She'd been trying to limit her alcohol intake — amongst everything else she'd been trying to do – but one wouldn't hurt. In any case, she was a couple of days past the peak. If it hadn't worked this time — and it hadn't worked the previous eighty-four times — the countdown would begin again for next month.

Alex rested a casual hand on her upper thigh, his own legs spread open wide as they always were, as if he was trying to pick up a breeze. In fairness, they'd tried everything else. He'd tackled the problem in his usual way: head in the sand. At least, that was how it had seemed to her. Where everyone else saw confidence and bravado, she saw a mask of avoidant behaviours. It was almost as if he saw it as a challenge; if his psychotherapist wife couldn't even spot it, how could anyone else?

Alex had always chosen his friends accordingly, and Sophie felt uncomfortable around many of them, but none more so than Charlie Ford. Why he still kept in touch with old school friends, regardless of what they'd become, she had no idea. She could only assume it was a combination of wanting to show off how well he'd done for himself and being able to feel young again, free of the burdens of adulthood and responsibility.

'Stuff going well then?' Charlie asked, avoiding the elephant in the room.

'Yeah, fine,' Sophie said, her stock answer.

'Really good, actually,' Alex said. 'New job's off to a blinder. I think we might have a few junior roles opening up if you fancy it?'

'Nah, I'm good,' Charlie replied.

'Things alright for you, then? Still in that hut by the A1?'

'It's a farmhouse. And yeah, same old same old. You know how it goes.'

'So what happened?' Alex said, after a short silence.

Charlie let out a sigh. 'I dunno. They were round at mine earlier, asking questions. Two of them. Plain clothes.'

'What did they want?'

'Wanted to know when I last saw him.'

'And what did you say?'

'The truth. That I was at the pub with him last night. What do you think I said?'

'I don't know, Charlie, do I? It's you. You could've said anything for all I know.'

'Can we just calm it down a bit?' Sophie said. 'We're all...

well, shocked by what's happened. The last thing we need is to be at each other's throats.'

Charlie rolled his tongue around the inside of his upper lip. 'Yeah, well I don't like the police, do I? Not exactly had the most functional and fruitful relationship over the years, know what I mean, doctor?'

'I'm not a doctor.'

'They think someone killed him,' Charlie said, looking at Alex.

'What's that meant to mean?'

'I dunno. But think about it. Look at it from their point of view. Yeah he'd had a few drinks, but that was Tom, wasn't it? He knew how to handle it. In any case, he was a happy drunk. Not the sort of bloke to go and top himself after a skinful.'

'Yeah, but they don't know that, do they?'

'They can find out. It's literally their job. They'll be talking to all of us, I imagine.'

Sophie shuffled in her seat. 'I haven't got anything to say.'

'Doesn't mean they won't ask it. Your folks still live in Manton?' Charlie asked Alex.

Alex leaned forward in his chair, propping his hand on his thigh, his elbow forming a perfect ninety-degree angle. 'And what's that meant to mean?'

'It was a question, dipshit.'

Alex held Charlie's gaze. 'So was mine.'

'It's where he died, ain't it? Just wondered if they might have seen or heard anything.'

'They didn't.'

'Alright. Police'll be doing door-to-door enquiries anyway, I imagine.'

'Good. Maybe it'll lead them to finding out if anyone else was involved. And if they were, I hope the guy swings for it.'

'Not the best choice of words,' Charlie said, taking a sip of his pint. 'Police seemed pretty certain someone else was involved, anyway.'

'And why wouldn't they? You were the last one to see him after all.'

'What do you mean by that?' Charlie asked.

'It was a question. Dipshit.'

'Can we just sit back and take a few moments?' Sophie said, raising a placating hand.

'What, so the guy with a rap sheet just happens to be the last person he talks to, and that automatically means I must've chucked him in my car, driven him down to Manton and lobbed him off a railway bridge?'

Sophie looked round, noticing a few of the other customers in the pub had clearly overheard their conversation. 'Guys, let's just take a step back for a minute, alright? Charlie, I'm sure Alex didn't mean anything by it. We're all... upset, I guess, by what's happened. Tempers and emotions are running high. But what's the point in getting at each other? It's not going to help anything. It's not going to bring Tom back. It's not what he would've wanted.'

'How do you know what he would've wanted?' Charlie said. 'You hardly ever bloody spoke to him.'

'You leave her out of this.'

'Or what?'

'What's going on?' a voice said from the doorway.

Sophie turned and saw Megan. She stood up and walked over, pulling her into a hug.

'Why's everyone angry?' Megan said.

'It's fine. Don't worry about it. How are you doing? I hope that's not a stupid question.'

Megan shrugged. 'I don't know how I'm meant to be doing. Sometimes my mind sort of clears for a minute or two, and then it just hits me again. I mean, I don't think anyone ever expects to be a widow at thirty-two, do they?'

'Oh for fuck's sake, you're not a widow,' Alex said. 'You were only together two months.'

'Three, actually. And as it happened we were very close.'

'Is there anyone you haven't been "very close" to? We went back twenty-odd years. You don't get to own grief.'

Sophie raised her hands. 'Can we just calm down, please? Anyway, where's Guy? Wasn't he meant to be here by now?'

'I was at school with you all too, you know,' Megan said, ignoring Sophie completely.

'You were at the *same* school. You didn't go to school *with* us. In case your memory has failed you, you were in the year below us and most of us had forgotten about you until two months ago.'

'Three!'

'Would anyone like a drink?' Sophie said, standing up.

Megan sighed and looked up at her. 'Yes. Thank you, Sophie. I think that'd be a very good idea.'

10

Caroline wondered if all therapists' treatment rooms looked so bland. Perhaps that was the whole idea: dull absolutely all sensory input to the point where you had no choice but to open up and reveal all your childhood trauma, like one of those 'absolute silence' sensory deprivation rooms, guaranteed to send anyone mad within twenty minutes.

She wondered how many people used the box of tissues that had been not-so-subtly placed on the coffee table; how many others had sat in this chair before her and counted every single leaf on the watercolour oak tree that hung on the wall opposite.

Rachel was only doing her job, but there was something in her over-soothing tone that almost bordered on patronising. One of Caroline's early jobs in the Met had been as a trained crisis negotiator. Tasked with talking suicidal people down from tall buildings, she was well aware of the psychological strategies and how they worked. Perhaps, she thought, that was why she was getting so riled having them used on her.

There were times when she'd wanted to yell *I'm a forty-some-thing professional! I don't need this bullshit!* but something else had come out instead. It was almost as if Rachel was one of those Indian snake charmers, gently playing her lilting and patronising flute, ever so softly coaxing the snakes out from within her.

And there were plenty of snakes. They hadn't even got to the dark, jet black ones; the ones that hissed in the night, their glands swollen with venom. It was inevitable that they'd get to that point someday. But someday could wait. For now, it was easy enough to let out some surface level stuff. It was a bit like opening a fizzy drink bottle that'd been shaken up beyond belief. Tight grip on the cap, let it open slowly, watch for the hiss and the bubbling then do it up again. Let a bit more out, tighten it back up before it bubbles over. Do that enough times, and the risk of an explosion was zero. She hoped therapy worked the same way.

'And how's work going?' Rachel asked. 'Is there a bit less pressure now?'

'In some ways, yeah. I mean, I've taken on a new case, but I think this one will be pretty straightforward. Can't really be any worse than the last one, anyway.'

'And how do you feel about that last one now?'

Caroline thought about this for a moment. 'I dunno. Kind of distant, I guess. Then again, I feel that way about lots of things. I suppose if I push them down far enough or create some mental distance there, it doesn't affect me so much.'

'But it's still there, isn't it?'

'Course. It's always there. Can't change that.'

'But we can change how we deal with things. Sometimes

it's best to tackle things head on. Note how we're feeling. Accept that as part of life and talk about it so we can move on properly. Otherwise, if we keep sweeping things under the carpet, the carpet becomes very difficult to walk on after a while. There'll be lumps and piles everywhere. You might get used to walking on it and adjusting your gait, but your furniture will look wonky and people will notice that. They might not know why, but something will seem a bit off, and not quite right. Does that make sense?'

'More than you know.'

'And let's face it, we all have dust. We all need to clean behind our furniture every now and again, or take the rug out for a good beating. None of us are immune from that. No-one lives in a dust-free house. Some people like to do a bit of cleaning each day, or perhaps once a week. Others let it build up a bit and do a big spring clean every now and again. I guess it's all personal preference, but little and often does tend to work best. Either way, the dust won't go away on its own. It'll just keep building and building.'

'That's why I tend to get Mark to do the housework.'

Rachel smiled. 'You use humour a lot, don't you?'

'Laugh or cry.'

'You mentioned Mark helping with the housework. Does he help with the other dusting? Do you ever speak to him and offload problems or discuss stuff that's troubling you?'

Caroline tensed her jaw. 'Not really. I mean, I don't really see the benefit in burdening him with stuff. He's got enough to deal with.'

Rachel nodded slowly. 'Okay. And if Mark had something which was really troubling him, really eating him up inside and causing him issues, would you want him to talk to you about it?'

'Well, yeah.'

'Why?'

Caroline swallowed. 'Because I wouldn't want him to feel alone. I'd want him to be able to share his troubles so we could work through them together.'

'And you wouldn't feel burdened by that?'

'Course not. It's what couples do.'

'But it's not what you do the other way round, is it? What makes you think Mark would feel burdened by your problems if you wouldn't feel burdened by his? Quite often, we worry too much about what other people think. There's a wise quote I heard once, actually. "You are not what you think you are. You are not what other people think you are. You are what you think other people think you are."'

'Yeah. I haven't had nearly enough coffee to decipher that one, I'm afraid.'

Rachel smiled. 'What I'm saying is you probably spend too much time worrying about what Mark would think. If there's no evidence that he'd feel burdened or not want you to share your problems with him, that's a concern you're fabricating. We all make our own realities. Our views on the world are entirely shaped by how we respond to events — not by the events themselves. You get to choose your emotions and your assumptions, and by that measure they can be changed too.'

'That thing I said about the coffee...'

'We'll get there,' Rachel said, smiling again. 'The mind has a wonderful way of altering our memories of what happened based purely on the emotions we felt at the time. Have you ever put on a piece of your favourite music, or played your favourite film, then after a couple of minutes thought you weren't in the mood for it? Perhaps the music didn't sound as good as it usually does, or the film wasn't doing it for you that time. That's your mind projecting its emotions. The song and the film aren't any worse or less good than they were the last time you heard or watched them. It's the same song, the same film. What's changed is your emotional state, and that makes you view the film or hear the song differently. You have a different perception of it. If that film or song were objectively good, or if the value you get from them was intrinsic, it would have had the same effect this time as it did the last. But it doesn't. So that reaction, those feelings — that reality — must come from inside you.'

'But what about things that actually *were* bad? Surely we can't just say that everything's in the mind.'

Rachel shook her head. 'No, I'm not saying that. Of course not. But the severity of it, and how much we let it play on our minds weeks, months, years later — that's all down to our minds. It's a form of self-torture.'

'And what if that self-torture is justified?'

'How do you mean?' Rachel asked, cocking her head.

'I mean, what if the thing that plagues you is something you deserve to be punished for? What if those years of mental torture are completely warranted?'

'Do you have an example?'

Caroline thought for a moment. Images flashed in front of her eyes, as clear and as vivid as they'd always been. Trapped inside her own mind, time provided no distance.

'No,' she said, eventually. 'No, I don't have an example.'

11

She arrived at work only an hour later than she otherwise would've done. Of course, she hadn't told work the reason why; the official excuse was that she had to do the school run because Mark had meetings. She wasn't sure how she was supposed to feel after a therapy session, but each time so far she'd come out feeling frustrated. Frustrated not with Rachel or the concept of therapy, but with her inability to have opened up, communicated and made the most of it.

She sat down in her office and ruminated on the fact this was costing her eighty quid a pop and wondered if it was worth it. Wine made her feel much better than therapy, and she could get a lot of wine for eighty quid. But she needed to do something. At least this way, it'd keep Mark happy that progress was being made.

A knock at the door made her jump.

'Come in.'

Sara Henshaw opened the door and stepped inside. 'Got

something you might be interested in. CCTV's back from the Horse and Jockey in Manton.'

'Excellent. Anything on it?'

'Yes and no. You might want to come and have a look at this.'

Caroline stood up and followed Sara to her desk, noticing the CCTV footage on her computer monitor.

'Right, here we are. Take a look at this.' Sara pressed a button on her keyboard and the video started to play.

There was nothing for a few seconds, then a Vauxhall Corsa came into view, before disappearing up Cemetery Lane. Ten minutes later, the same vehicle came back in the other direction.

'Wow. Okay. Is that the only car?' Caroline asked.

'Yep. Nothing else went that way, or came from that way, until our boys turned up shortly after six o'clock.'

'So that's got to be our killer. Can we see how many people are in the car? Registration number?'

Sara shook her head. 'No, the lighting's awful. I can ask to have it worked on and see if we might be able to pick up a partial plate, but I'm not hopeful. You can barely make out what type of car it is. It's only because it's such a distinctive shape.'

'And pretty common, too,' Caroline said. 'How many of those are in Rutland? Must be hundreds.'

'Could even be from one of the surrounding counties. It's going to be almost impossible.'

'Christ. Find out if there's any other registered CCTV in the area, too. Maybe get uniform to take a walk around and see if there's any residential cameras. Someone will have picked the car up in better quality than this. Maybe we can get at least a partial registration from one of those. That'll narrow it down massively.'

Caroline looked at the screen and watched the car again. It was impossible to see who was driving or even how many people were in the car. Was Tom Medland a willing passenger, or was he unconscious — or worse — and shoved in the boot? There was no way they could know. The footage was too grainy, the frame rate was too slow and any moving objects were blurred beyond belief. But there was no mistaking the model of car. And there was no mistaking the fact that Caroline was looking directly at their killer.

12

The inevitable day-two slowdown had well and truly kicked in, but Caroline was more than used to that by now. When she was in the Met, this was the point at which they'd open up the investigation further and spend time speaking to wider circles of friends, work colleagues and acquaintances of the victim. With such a small team in Rutland, though, they had to prioritise. That wasn't necessarily a bad thing. Reduced numbers meant everyone knew the details, and a laser-tight focus enabled them to get into the nuts and bolts of the investigation.

She'd never been the sort of person to take her work home with her — most police officers weren't — but she'd found it occupying more of her headspace since she'd begun heading up murder investigations here. She felt the burden of responsibility far more than she had working as part of a much larger team in London. She supposed that was natural, and it was something she was going to have to come to terms with.

She and Mark had spent the evening watching a film, and

were now half-watching a travel documentary about Thailand, which had come on after. It wasn't an area of the world she'd ever been to, or which had ever appealed to her, but it wasn't particularly challenging viewing, and that was exactly what she needed right now.

Winding down wasn't something that came easily to her, but with the clock nudging half-past eleven at night, she was at least starting to feel as though it might be time to head to bed.

The chemotherapy left her swinging between feeling tired and lethargic, and having strange bursts of energy, almost as if her body was saving it up and using it all in one go. It took some getting used to, and she'd learned to take it a little easier even when she felt like she could conquer the world. That way, the inevitable slumps would be more manageable when they came.

'I might head up,' Mark said, as if he'd read her mind.

As he stood up, Caroline noticed something she hadn't even thought about for a long time. She didn't know whether it was the wine speaking or the gradual clearing of her mind, but in that moment she found Mark almost irresistibly attractive. She stood too, and pulled him in close, kissing him.

'Does that mean you're coming up with me?' he asked.

Caroline shook her head. 'Oh no. No, I'm not going anywhere. And more to the point,' she said, pushing him down on the sofa, 'neither are you.'

13

They finally got to bed just after one o'clock in the morning. The sound of her alarm at seven o'clock had been the last noise she'd wanted to hear, but a couple of strong coffees had seen her on the road to some sort of coherent thought. By the time she left the house, she'd perked right up and was feeling brighter than she had in a long time.

'Christ, you look like shit,' Dexter said as she walked into the office.

'Good morning to you too. In that case, I think I'll start with coffee.'

'Great idea. Milk and one, please.'

Caroline looked at Dexter and laughed. Workplace banter was something she'd missed. It had been gradually ironed out in the Met, but she'd been pleased to see it was still alive and well in Rutland, even if Dexter did push the limits occasionally. Still, he was the only one who could get away with it.

She headed for the kitchenette and put the kettle on, then

leaned against the work surface and scrolled through her emails on her phone. A few moments later, Dexter came in.

'Might want to pop that kettle off.'

'Why's that?'

'It might be nothing, but there's been a report of a body out near Lyndon. Given what happened in Manton recently, we should take a look.'

'Christ. Suspicious?'

'On the face of it, no. Suicide written all over it. But it's another young male, and another hanging. Something about it doesn't feel right. In fact, it feels very, very wrong.'

Caroline swallowed and noticed her heart rate increasing. She didn't want to admit it, but a rising dread in the pit of her stomach told her she had to agree.

14

'What are they building here?' Caroline asked as they approached the construction site where the body had been found.

'A luxury spa hotel and resort, apparently. One of those places where you get to eat seaweed and have your face rubbed with an organic Rutland Water trout.'

'Sounds... nice.'

'Sounds expensive, more like. It's costing them millions to build. Dread to think what the prices will be like when it's open.'

They parked up and showed their ID to PC Karina Gallagher, the officer at the entrance to the site, who updated them on what had happened.

'One of the builders found him hanging from the scaffolding. Someone said he's the architect who designed the place, but we haven't had confirmation of that yet.'

Caroline swallowed. 'What's the name of the construction company?'

'Bowes. Why's that?'

'Just checking. Has anyone interfered with the body?'

'The guy who found him pulled him down, thinking he might be able to resuscitate him but there's no chance. He was long gone by that point. You'd have more of a chance trying to revive Tutankhamun.'

'Was there a note? Any form of positive ID?'

'No note. Only ID is eyewitnesses saying they recognised him.'

'How many?'

'Two,' Gallagher said, walking them through the site to the location of the body.

'They're probably right, then. What's the architect's name?'

'Guy Sherman.'

'Did they know him well?'

Gallagher shook her head. 'Only by sight. The owner's on his way, apparently. He might know a bit more.'

Caroline looked at the body of the man they assumed to be Guy Sherman, and couldn't help but notice the parallels between him and Tom Medland. They were a similar age and of a similar build. It was true to say they were in the right demographic for the majority of suicides, but the timing and level of coincidence wasn't lost on Caroline.

'You thinking what I'm thinking?' Dexter asked her.

'I'm trying not to. Sorry, can you give us a sec please?' she asked PC Gallagher, watching as she walked back to the entrance to the site.

'Hell of a coincidence, isn't it?' Dexter said.

'Yeah. At the moment, that's exactly what it is. We don't

even know for certain Tom Medland was murdered. Those tyre marks could've been anything. Joy riders, someone taking a short cut.'

'And what about all the foliage and bracken and stuff that'd been flattened down?'

'Could be kids messing around. Animals, even. Tom had no mud or dirt on his clothing, no rips or tears, nothing. If he'd been dragged down that bank, it'd be even clearer from looking at him than at the bank, but there was nothing. And this one? Doesn't seem to be anything suspicious at all. He works here. Knew no-one would be around at night. Construction's a brutal game. He could've been under all sorts of pressure. Bullying, perhaps. Daft "banter" that got out of hand over the weeks and months? Maybe he wanted his colleagues to find him. Wanted them to see it. Until we get a positive ID and find out more about him, we won't know. Know the victim, Dex. That's always the first priority. Then everything else tends to fall into place.'

Before Dexter could reply, Caroline noticed Karina Gallagher walking towards them again.

'The owner's here,' she said. 'I've told him he can't come on site just yet, but did you want to have a word?'

'I'll let you deal with him, if that's okay. If he's able to give us a positive ID and details for his next of kin, we'll go and see the family.'

Caroline looked back at the body of the man they assumed to be Guy Sherman and frowned at the horrors — whether internal or external — that had plagued him in his final moments.

15

Whilst Caroline relayed what they'd discovered to Sara and Aidan in the incident room, the site owner Owen Samuels confirmed the body as that of Guy Sherman, his architect. They'd need his family to identify the body officially, but Owen's identification meant they could at least inform the family with a strong level of certainty.

Caroline remembered a story she'd been told during her training, in which a dead body had been positively identified by a close friend. The officers had gone to tell the man's wife her husband had sadly died whilst popping out to the shops, only for her heart wrenching sobs to be halted by the husband strolling in through the back door with a selection of Tesco's carrier bags.

For Guy Sherman, though, there was no wife. He lived alone in a small rented house in Oakham, although his parents lived on a new estate on the northern side of Uppingham. Keith and Janet Sherman had taken the news particularly badly, with Guy's father sitting in stunned silence as Caroline told them what little they knew about their son's death.

'I just... I keep wanting to phone him and prove he's fine,' Janet said, her eyes red raw. 'I just... I can't get my head round it. It can't be true. It can't.'

Caroline watched as she broke down again, another wave of grief hitting her like a freight train.

'What was Guy's mental state? Had he expressed any intentions to self-harm at all?'

Janet shook her head. 'No. Not at all. He was doing well. He lived down in Bristol after finishing university and came back up here when he got the job working on the spa resort at Lyndon. Things were really looking up for him. The owner was really pleased with what he'd done, and said he wanted to use Guy for some other plans he had. He was thinking of buying his own place up here and everything.'

'Did he own a house in Bristol?' Caroline asked.

'Yes. He designed it himself. Beautiful, it was.'

'Tell them the truth, Janet,' her husband said, his voice almost a murmur. They were the first words Caroline and Dexter had heard him say.

'Keith. Please,' came his wife's response.

'What do you mean?' Caroline asked.

Keith let out a gentle sigh. 'We found out he'd sold the place to one of these buyback firms. Dodgy property investors who buy your house at a knockdown price and rent it back to you.'

'Why would he do that?'

'Because he had no money and no bugger would buy the place.'

'He didn't want to leave it. It was his baby,' Janet said.

'He left it quickly enough when the job in Lyndon cropped up. Place was all glass and sheet metal. Who wants to spend three quarters of a million quid on a prefab garage?'

'Was he in financial difficulty?' Caroline asked, noticing Dexter's intrigue growing.

'No, he was fine. One of those things,' Janet said.

'Stone broke,' Keith said, correcting her. 'Look, my wife's not going to tell you the truth, so I might as well. Guy was a drinker. An alcoholic. Christ knows how much he's spunked up the wall over the years. What wasn't locked away in that luxury portakabin down in Bristol was tucked safely away in the pub's till.'

Janet stood and left the room. Keith sighed.

'I'll go after her in a bit,' he said. 'I'm sorry. She can't handle facing up to what Guy had become. To tell you the truth, I had half a feeling we'd get a knock on the door one day to say he'd got in a fight or fallen over drunk and hit his head. But what can we do? We offered to take him in, said we'd put a roof over his head. We've got plenty of space here. But he wouldn't have any of it. Couldn't admit he had a problem. He didn't do failure, see. That's how he saw it. Failure.'

'Did he ever show any sign of wanting to end his life? Any spells of depression?'

Keith shook his head then shrugged. 'You never know what's going on inside someone's head, do you? I mean, anything's possible, but he always seemed so chipper.'

'Did he have many friends?' Caroline asked, noticing that he was talking much more freely now the initial shock had settled — and since his wife had left the room.

'Depends what you mean by friends, really. He had a lot of acquaintances, let's put it that way, but he was always a loner at heart.'

'What do you mean by acquaintances?'

'People he'd see down the pub, that sort of thing.'

'Did he have a regular watering hole?'

'Oh, he wasn't fussy. He'd go all over. He'd usually be down at The Vaults, though. Think he was friendly with a few of the regulars in there. He used to catch up with some old school friends occasionally, but that was about it. Other than that, he didn't really see many people. That was his life. Jesus Christ, it's horrible talking about him like this. I still can't...'

'Had he had many fallings out with people?' Caroline asked.

'No... Not that I'm aware of. He wasn't the sort of person who fell out with anyone. He kept himself to himself, you know? Always bright and bubbly enough with people, but no-one ever got close to him. Almost as if it was an act of some sort. Bloody talented architect, though. Apparently. If you like that sort of thing. I'd better just... Y'know.' Keith gestured in the direction of the hallway and Caroline nodded that he should go after Janet.

'Bit weird that, isn't it?' Dexter asked, whispering.

Caroline murmured her agreement. If Guy had been intent on ending his own life, why had he gone all the way to the top of the building and then hanged himself? Why not just throw himself off the top and to his certain death? It clearly wasn't a cry for help, else he would've done it at a time when someone else could've found him, rather than waiting until everyone had gone home. It didn't add up. And that was what worried her the most.

16

Both Caroline and Dexter had a distinct feeling that something wasn't quite right. Each of Guy's parents seemed to have completely different views on what had happened. His mum seemed convinced he'd been doing well and had no reason to want to end his own life, but his dad had been far more cautious on that front. The revelations about Guy's financial affairs and his heavy drinking were things they'd need to follow up far more thoroughly, and Caroline updated the rest of the team once they were back in the incident room.

She was keen to ensure all bases were covered, but without pushing the fact she thought they might have a double murderer on their hands.

'SOCOs say there are some fibres under his fingernails, which they think probably match the rope he was hanged with. Now, that could be a sign that he fought back and struggled when the noose was round his neck, but it's also entirely possible that he simply changed his mind. It's not uncommon for that to happen, to say the least. At this moment in time, there are no reasons to suspect that anyone was responsible for Guy Sherman's death other than himself. And we're still a long, long way from ruling that out when it comes to Tom Medland, too.'

Even though all possibilities were swilling round in her mind, she had to place her team's efforts on the most likely scenario. But even she couldn't deny that there was a large element of wishful thinking in this. The last time there'd been a double murder in Rutland, she'd been kicked off the case and it'd been handed over to EMSOU, the East Midlands Special Operations Unit. She couldn't risk this happening again. Even one confirmed murder would prick the ears of those higher up and force her to hand the case over.

'Sorry to burst that bubble,' Aidan said, looking at his computer screen, 'but the initial post-mortem results are back on Tom Medland.'

'Go on,' Caroline said, knowing she could digest the contents of the email fully once she was back at her desk and had opened her copy.

'In short, and in English, there's some potential evidence he was dead prior to being hanged. There's a small amount of lividity, or blood pooling, which shows he might've been killed while in a seated position. Apparently it's only very mild, but enough to have been noticeable and worth pointing out.'

'Enough to stand up in court?'

Aidan shrugged. 'No idea. They didn't seem to think it was conclusive, but it's a pretty good starting point. Their main point of concern was bruising around his neck which they said showed he'd been strangled prior to being hanged. They were much more certain of that. Whichever way we look at it, I think we can safely say Tom was murdered and then hanged.'

Caroline swallowed. 'Right. Thanks, Aidan.'

'Guv,' Sara said. 'Just a quick one. Might be nothing, but I noticed Tom and Guy were only about six weeks apart, age-wise. I checked, and they both went to the same school so would've been in the same year. It's a pretty big school, so it doesn't necessarily mean anything, but might be something we want to look at in a bit more detail and see if they knew each other.'

'Good spot, Sara. Well done. Let's speak to the families. Check Tom and Guy's Facebook profiles, see if they were friends on there. I imagine they probably were, if they were in the same year at school. Cross-reference with phone contacts. See if they called or texted each other.'

Her team nodded. And in that moment, Caroline felt they were making real progress.

17

Sophie Lawson watched on as Alex fired another goal into the back of the net, the computer-generated players celebrating on the screen in front of him. He'd never been good at dealing with negative emotions, and tended to push them to one side. But she was sure his cold exterior might crack on hearing of the death of two of his friends.

'Are we even going to talk about this?' she said as the referee's whistle blew and Alex tapped away at the controller as the game restarted.

'Talk about what?'

'What do you think? Tom and Guy.'

'What's the point? Talking about them isn't going to bring them back, is it?'

'No, but it's not normal to react like this, is it?'

'Like what?'

'Just going and playing a computer game.'

Alex paused the game and looked up at her. 'Alright, so what is normal? Tell me, how are you meant to react when two of your friends die in the space of two days? I didn't realise there was some "normal" way to react to that.'

Sophie shuffled from one foot to the other. 'I just mean... Do you even care?'

'Course I do. But come on. We were close, but we're all busy adults now. We'd barely spoken to Tom in god knows how long. And Guy was always going to chuck himself into an early grave. He was always the outsider. What good's it going to do for us to start moping around? The police will do what they've got to do. Until then, PMA.'

'What?'

'Positive mental attitude. Look forward, not back. You can't change stuff that's already happened,' he said, returning to his game.

Sophie didn't know who seemed more robotic — her husband, or the computer-generated footballers on the screen in front of him.

'Aren't you even... worried?' she asked.

'About what?'

'Well, I mean, it's a bit of a coincidence, isn't it? Two of the group, both in the same week.'

'What "group"? There is no group.'

'You know what group. What if it's... What if they didn't kill themselves?'

Alex stayed silent for a moment, not taking his eyes off the game. 'They did,' he said eventually. 'They did.'

18

One of the things Caroline loved most about her husband was that he always knew the right thing to say and do, even if she didn't see it that way at the time. With the benefit of hindsight, she realised he rarely got it wrong. So although she wanted nothing more than to get home after work and go straight to bed, she couldn't help but feel even more in love with Mark as he told her he'd organised a babysitter for the evening and was taking her out for dinner and drinks.

As they walked into town that evening, Caroline felt the warmth of the end of the day's sun on her face, and wondered how many more evenings like this there'd be. Summer always seemed to disappear so quickly; not like the ones she'd known as a kid, which seemed to stretch out for months and years. Those were the experiences Josh and Archie were having now, and she felt a pang of guilt as she realised she was missing large chunks of them.

Mark had booked a table at 10 Dining Street, a restaurant which had nothing to do with politics and was actually on the corner of John Street and New Street, but which had been designed on the outside to look like the Prime Minister's London residence. Although they didn't get to go out for dinner much, takeaways were an almost weekly occurrence, and 10 Dining Street was often their restaurant of choice.

The wonderful aroma of spices and curried meats had Caroline's stomach rumbling before they'd even walked through the famous black door, and she'd found it hard to narrow down what she wanted from the menu.

With starters out of the way, she'd begun to relax — something Mark had clearly noticed.

'So how are the sessions going?' he asked. 'With Rachel, I mean.'

'Yeah, alright, I think,' Caroline said, not wanting to tell him she didn't feel she was getting much from them, other than frustration. 'It takes time, though. It's not an instant thing. Some people go for years.'

'Ouch. Sounds expensive.'

'Good job we won't be spending too much on drinks tonight then, eh?' she replied with a smile.

'Sorry about that.'

Caroline laughed. 'It's fine. We can get a drink somewhere else afterwards.'

'The worst thing is I knew they didn't serve alcohol, but just completely forgot. I'll chalk it up to old age.'

'Honestly, don't worry. Sara tipped me off about a place in town. A hidden gem, apparently.'

'Sara's organisational skills strike again, eh?'

'Dexter calls her Miss Filofax,' Caroline said, laughing.

Mark smiled. 'You seem happier.'

She thought about this for a moment, watching as Mark tucked into his main course. She was at an odd juncture, but didn't quite know how best to explain that. Telling Mark and the boys about her illness had provided a huge sense of relief, but there were still things that worried her greatly. Things were moving, but there was still a long road ahead of her and more than a few things she was going to need to address.

Once the meal was over, the pair ambled slowly towards home, Mark having forgotten all about Caroline's mention of drinks. As they walked up Church Street, she led him down a path that ran down the side of the church, and which headed towards the Market Place.

'Wouldn't it be quicker to carry on up the road?' Mark asked.

'Nope. Come on.'

She led him down the narrow path and towards a door which led into a beautiful garden, which had been decorated in fairytale cottage style and decked out with lights. She could see a bar at the end of the garden, beyond the cast-iron tables and seating, where a number of people were enjoying evening drinks in the later summer warmth at Castle Cottage.

'I never knew this was here,' Mark said, amazed.

'Me neither,' Caroline said. 'I guess that's why it's called a hidden gem.'

Two hours later, and feeling much more relaxed than she had in a long time, Caroline and Mark headed home and to bed. Although she might have felt relaxed on the outside, her dreams that night proved her mind was anything other than at ease.

19

It always began with the sound of the plane. A turboprop, its pilot taking in the stunning scenery and incredible weather. Next, water lashing over the rocks, swirling and pooling. Laughter. The smell of sun-kissed asphalt and the faint scent of lavender. The occasional taste of iron after an unexpected dunking. The images were always the last to appear. Topless, tanned boys. The white of the water as it careened over the rocks, the warm glow of the sun in the azure sky. Slowly, it appeared. But before that it was darkness. Her opening montage; his final moments.

The memories resurfacing were gradual, building and growing each time. But the moment it happened had been more akin to someone flicking a switch. There was no slow build-up, no gradual realisation of what was happening. One moment it had been the perfect summer's day. The sort of montage that lasts a lifetime. Glorious memories being etched in for eternity. Then it happened.

Harry's eyes were as clear as day. She was still there, looking into them. She rolled his name around her mouth, having learnt it only an hour earlier. For four days until then, he'd been The Boy From Plot 22. The boy whose parents spent their days on the campsite drinking lager from a can while their only son sat reading books.

It was the books that had drawn her to him. She'd never been a big reader, but had heard people talk about the magic of it. She'd sit and watch him, wondering what sort of magic he was experiencing, gazing on as his crystal blue eyes danced over the pages. Once or twice, he caught her looking and smiled, before returning to his magical experience.

She hadn't expected their first conversation to happen by the toilet block, but that was the way the universe had ordained it. When she told The Boy From Plot 22 that she and her brother Stuart were going to play down by the river, a part of her hoped he might ask if he could join them. But she'd never expected he actually would.

She'd walked behind him, watching his hair bounce just above his shoulders as they made their way down the rocky path to the river. There was one part that was like a free jacuzzi, the water cascading over the rocks in such a way that it roiled and bubbled under the surface. She'd never had any interest in boys before The Boy From Plot 22. Harry. She felt his name again now, tasted it.

His eyes burned into hers as he told her about his love for literature, how he'd gradually worked his way through almost the entire fiction section at the library. It seemed so otherworldly to her. He seemed wise well beyond his twelve years, talking to her about his recent discovery of the great romantic poets. For all she knew it could have been complete bullshit, but she didn't care. She was happy just to listen and be lost in his enthusiasm as the water bubbled around them, washing over the rocks and down the stream.

Then the switch flipped.

It was Harry who noticed first. She looked at him as his features dropped and horror crossed his face. Caroline turned to follow his gaze. Before her conscious brain had even worked out what was going on, her instinctive reactions kicked in. She tried to run through the water but stumbled, her legs unable to move quickly enough to make progress. She watched as Stuart's face grew evermore panicked, the flowing river enveloping him as he tried to struggle free.

The words of her mother: Make sure you keep an eye on Stuie! He's only six! You know he's not a strong swimmer!

The reply of hers: Don't worry, Mum! I will!

Caroline clambered over the rocks, feeling her shins scrape against their hard face, her ankle jarring as she desperately scrambled to reach him.

She knew what had happened before she noticed the movement stop. Something settled and the world became After. There was no going back.

She dragged Stuart to the shore, his limp, empty body bearing more weight than it had in life. She fought to resuscitate him, trying as hard as she could to remember what she'd seen on TV. Chest compressions. Mouth to mouth. Something about the Bee Gees. She continued and continued, all the while knowing there was no hope. No point. No need.

She looked up and over at the river, and saw nothing. She

looked then further along the bank and thought she saw movement in the back of the trees. But nothing else.

The Boy From Plot 22 was gone. Stuart was gone. Everything was gone. Now it was After. And all that remained was the sound of the plane.

20

Caroline woke the next morning feeling like she'd been hit by a freight train. The dream came occasionally, but never as vividly as it had last night.

'You okay?' Mark asked when she got downstairs.

'Yeah, you?'

'I'm alright. You were thrashing around in your sleep again.'

'Sorry. Curry and alcohol. Never a good combination for me.'

'Made you an extra-strong coffee. You'll be thrashing about again in no time.'

Caroline kissed her husband on the cheek and devoured the hot black liquid, not caring whether she burnt her mouth. In many ways, it would be welcome. Deserved, perhaps.

The fog had started to lift a little by the time she got to work, and she could almost have predicted that this sense of growing ease would be punctured by the arrival of Chief Superintendent Derek Arnold.

'Have you got a sec?' he asked, before walking back to his own office, leaving her with no chance to respond in the negative. She followed him, and sat down in the seat he pointed to, even though it was the only other one in the room.

'You okay?' he said, looking at her properly for the first time. 'You look dreadful.'

'Yeah, I'm fine. Just a restless night.'

'Stress?'

Caroline thought for a moment before answering. 'No. No, fine on that front. Mark and I went out for a heavy meal last night. Never sleep well after that.'

He nodded and steepled his hands. 'What are your thoughts on Thomas Medland and Guy Sherman?'

'In what respect, sir?'

'In respect of their deaths. Are they both being treated as suspicious?'

Caroline swallowed. 'We're investigating them as such, but they're technically open in the absence of further forensic evidence and full pathology results. We're continuing to investigate the possibility of foul play, particularly in the case of Tom Medland, but at the moment we've no reason to believe there's anything suspicious about the death of Guy Sherman.'

'Apart from the fact he knew Thomas Medland, whose death you are suspicious about, and that he died in the exact same way.'

'There are crucial differences. Besides, we can't discount the possibility that Guy killed himself because he was upset at Tom's death. Far from it. Plus we've discovered he had a history of financial difficulties and struggles with alcohol dependency. There's an awful lot that leads us to believe Guy Sherman did kill himself.'

'Mmmmm. Almost too convenient, in fact, no?'

Caroline shook her head. 'I wouldn't say so, no. In fact it's pretty textbook.'

'Precisely. That's what makes me feel very uneasy about it all.'

Caroline watched him, not wanting to say anything. She had to admit those thoughts — and more — had crossed her mind on more than one occasion, although she dearly hoped she was wrong. 'Well we should hear more back soon. We're waiting on pathology results on Guy Sherman. If there's any suggestion whatsoever of foul play, we'll be able to jump right on it.'

'You'll need resources.'

'We'll manage. More than manage, in fact. I'm lucky to have a fantastic team.'

Arnold sighed. 'Look, I've got to be mindful of your welfare. It's part of the job, as you well know.'

'My welfare?'

'You know. The... You know.'

'Cancer.'

'Yes. That.'

'I see no reason why that would cause an issue. I presume you're not trying to shepherd me out because I've got an illness?'

'Oh god, no. No, not in the slightest. Christ, please don't think that. Or say that. Like I say, I'm trying to look out for you and make sure you're supported in the best way possible.'

'I am. I couldn't ask for a better team than the one I've got.'

'And I'm not suggesting I take that away from you. I'm suggesting we add to it.'

'How so?'

'With the support of EMSOU.'

'Support? Or do you mean you want to transfer the case over to them?'

'This isn't an "us and them" scenario, Caroline. The only "us and them" are the police and the criminals. EMSOU are on your side. I'm on your side. We all want to make sure whoever's responsible for this is brought to justice.'

'And if they're both deemed to be suicides?'

Arnold leaned back in his chair, which creaked slightly as he did so. 'Well, then you'd better damn well hope that's the case, hadn't you?'

21

Shortly after she arrived back in the office, Dexter knocked on her door and entered. 'Everything alright?'

'Fine, Dex. What's up?'

'The suicide angle. I've been doing a bit of research, looking into suicide pacts. Do you remember the Bridgend thing in Wales a few years ago? Twenty-six young people in Bridgend killed themselves in the space of two years.'

'Well, yeah. Have you ever been to Bridgend?'

'In the ten years prior to that, the average in the town was three a year,' Dexter said, ignoring her barb. 'They reckon there's been more since and that we're up to seventy-nine now. The police have asked the media to stop reporting them, because each time they do, more happen.'

'I'm vaguely familiar with it. There wasn't any suspicion of foul play, though, was there?'

'Not really, no. But it seemed to be something that grew in popularity each time someone did it. It became this sort of horrible magnet.'

'Why, though?' Caroline said. 'What's the appeal?'

Dexter shrugged. 'I don't think it's an appeal so much as young people being desperate and depressed and seeing others taking that way out. Maybe there's a bit of legendary status about it. Bit like the 27 Club.'

'27 Club?'

'Yeah. Loads of famous musicians and artists died at the age of twenty-seven. Jimi Hendrix, Janis Joplin, Jim Morrison, Amy Winehouse, Kurt Cobain. They were all twenty-seven when they died. It's an almost mythical way to go. I guess we're all going to die one day. Being able to control it and go out in style as part of a lasting fable isn't the worst way to go.'

Caroline shifted in her chair. 'But there isn't a fable or legend here. Not in Rutland. This isn't Bridgend. It's not the 27 Club. We can't go around saying Guy Sherman killed himself because of a growing cult, when there was only one person in it at that point.'

'No, but they all start somewhere, don't they?'

'I dunno,' Caroline said, shaking her head. 'I still think we're looking at potentially suspicious circumstances in the death of Tom Medland, and suicide for Guy Sherman. We can't discount the possibility of Guy being Tom's killer, either.'

'Then topping himself before we catch him?'

'It's possible. It needs looking into. We need to look at Guy more closely. Know the victim. Let's go into more detail. Find out where he was on the night Tom Medland died. See what car or cars he owned. Any luck tracing the Corsa?'

Dexter shook his head. 'Not yet. It took ages to pull a list off. We've contacted owners' clubs, too, just to make sure we've got all bases covered. Sara's going through the list as we speak. We're also trying to get phone triangulation for anyone who might've been in the area around the time Tom died. If we can get a match, we'll have a suspect.'

'But nothing yet?'

'Nothing yet. At some point we have to look at the possibility that the tyre tracks and flattened weeds were just a coincidence.'

Caroline looked at Dexter and smiled. 'No such thing, Dex. There's something here. I know there is. We just need to work out what.'

22

Sometimes, Caroline despaired at people. The idea that someone would invest millions of pounds into a brand new spa hotel complex and not spend a couple of hundred quid on securing the site with CCTV was phenomenal. Untold damage could be caused even before the complex was built, and with so much valuable machinery on site, she was amazed the owner hadn't taken at least basic security precautions. It was nothing unusual, though. She saw it all the time. Million-pound houses without an alarm, people wandering round town with Rolex watches on their wrists. It was as if they were so far removed from the sorts of people who were targeting them, they were unable to even see they *were* the targets.

Caroline's strong instinct told her something strange was at play — as much as she didn't want to admit it to herself.

She knew many cases didn't necessarily hinge on what *could* be proved, but instead often pivoted on what *couldn't*. They couldn't prove that no-one else visited the building site after Guy arrived, or that he was on his own. He would've had unfettered access any time he liked as the project's architect. What was to say someone hadn't broken into the site and killed him? SOCO's initial findings said otherwise, of course, but Caroline just couldn't shake the feeling something was missing.

They needed more information on Guy. Even if he had killed himself, there was a reason he chose that spot. And Caroline knew there was one person who might be able to help them find those answers.

23

Owen Samuels's house in Egleton was much as Caroline had expected it to be: swanky, grandiose and — dare she say it — a little over the top. He was clearly a man who'd made some money, but he seemed pleasant enough.

'Nice place you've got here,' she said, as they sat down in his huge kitchen.

'Thank you. A bit much for one person at times, but it makes for a handy bachelor pad. The original house is actually much smaller, but I had it extended heavily and brought up to date. I think they've done a great job.'

'They have. Is that your game, then? Building and development?'

'Not really, no. I like to have my fingers in quite a few pies, as it happens. I began by building startups and selling them on. Then I started rescuing struggling companies by buying them out, fixing their problems and making them profitable before selling them on too. Lots of people think business is difficult, but it really isn't. Most of the time, the same rules apply across the board. A lot of people don't realise that. It's only complicated if you make it complicated. The thing about business is you can happily fail nine times out of ten. You only need to strike it lucky once and everything changes. Invest that wisely, make another couple of good decisions and you're set up for life.'

'What sort of businesses?' Caroline asked, keen to engage him in conversation and win his trust.

'Oh, all sorts. I'm into leisure and tourism at the moment, mostly. Especially around here. But I've got interests in retail, marketing, interior design, garages, robotics, print — you name it.'

'Blimey. And there's me thinking print's dead.'

'It is if you think it's the same type of print it's always been. Industries don't die. They evolve. The only things that die are businesses that don't evolve and adapt with them.'

'Interesting stuff. You probably know why we're here, Mr Samuels. Can you tell us a little more about how you know Guy Sherman?' Caroline asked.

Owen leaned back in his chair. 'Well, we probably first met a year or two ago. I was looking for an architect for the new spa hotel and someone mentioned Guy's name. They said he was local but had moved away, but I thought he might like to work on a project on his native patch. So I got in touch with him. He seemed like one of life's geniuses. He just sort of "got" what I was looking for, do you know what I mean? Sometimes you just click with a person and realise they've got the same ideas and goals as you have. Pure gold dust in this industry. He was the best in the business if you ask me.'

'You got on well, then?'

'Very well. In fact, I committed to using him for every-thing I do. I've got big plans, and I wanted Guy at the heart of them all.'

'What sort of plans?' Dexter asked.

'Tourism, mainly. Staycationing is huge at the moment, and growing all the time. I'm talking spa hotels, glamping, boating. Rutland's perfect for all that. Right in the centre of the country, miles of beautiful open water, nice affluent area. And largely untouched.'

'That won't last for long if you build all over it, though, will it?' Caroline said.

'Oh no, I don't intend to do that. Far from it. That was the whole reason I employed Guy. I wanted everything to be done very ethically, and without simply concreting over everything. I'm a big believer in morals and doing the right thing. Sustain-ably sourced materials, local contractors, local employees.'

Caroline nodded and looked around her. It was clear his approach had worked up until now, at least. 'And when did you last see Guy?'

'That's the worrying thing. I think I was probably the last person to see him alive. We had a meeting at the spa resort site. Everyone else had gone home by the time we were done, and Guy said he wanted to take a look at one of the views from the scaffolding. I had another meeting at seven p.m. so I left him to it and headed off. That was the last I saw of him.'

'When did you leave?' Caroline asked.

'About six forty-five, I reckon. The meeting was at the Exeter Arms in Barrowden and I didn't want to be late.'

'Was there any sign that Guy was depressed or upset?'

'No, nothing at all. That's the scariest thing about it. Our meeting was very positive. We discussed how the build had progressed and how it was shaping up, I talked him through preliminary plans I had for other projects, and when I left he was smiling. I had absolutely no idea what was about to happen. It's come as a huge shock.'

Caroline knew from experience that truly suicidal people often did an incredible job of hiding their intentions from their friends and loved ones. Did that indicate the deaths of Tom and Guy weren't connected? On the face of it, it didn't seem so. But at the same time she had a horrible sinking feeling that all wasn't as it seemed.

24

The first thing Sophie wanted to complain about was the fact the others had got to The Grainstore first and chosen a table outside. The sun was up now, but in half an hour it'd be freezing cold, and she hadn't brought a jumper. If only Alex had been ready on time — or before — they could have got there earlier and chosen a table inside.

'How're you doing, Megan?' Sophie asked, still feeling awkward about what had been said the other night.

'I'm okay. Just trying to sort of get on as best I can, you know?'

'Can't imagine it's easy.'

'Does feel a bit weird all meeting up without Tom and Guy,' Charlie said. 'It's meant to be the big summer pub crawl.'

Alex let out a petulant sigh. 'That would've been Saturday. Besides which, it's not *weird*, is it? It'd be even weirder if they were here, seeing as they're both stone dead.'

'Alex!' Sophie shrieked.

'It's okay,' Megan said, the effects of a glass or two of wine already evident. 'To be fair, he's got a point.' She looked at Alex and laughed, her acceptance defusing the situation immediately. Sometimes, dark humour was the only way through it.

The easy feeling didn't last for long, though. Half an hour later, just as the sun disappeared over the top of the train station and Sophie started to shiver, the conversation turned darker.

'Doesn't it worry you?' Charlie asked in a conspiratorial tone.

'What?' Alex replied.

'That two people we know have died recently.'

'We all die eventually. Bit difficult to time it so we're all nice and evenly spaced out, isn't it?'

Sophie gave Alex an icy stare, but he wasn't looking at her.

'Come on, mate. Drop the act,' Charlie said.

'It's fine,' Megan said. 'We're all upset. I'm sure Alex didn't mean anything by it.'

Sophie thought for a moment she noticed a look in Megan's eye when she looked at Alex. She shuffled towards him and put her hand on his upper thigh, claiming him. Megan Wilkes had worked her way around most of the group over the years, but she still hadn't been able to get her grubby little mitts on Alex, as much as Sophie was sure she wanted to. Why was Megan even here, anyway? She was never part of the group. Not properly. She clung on occasionally whenever she was sleeping with one of the lads, but she wasn't one of them. She had no reason to be here, other than to act the part of the grieving girlfriend. Little bitch even had the nerve to call herself a widow — as if Tom would've got married to *that*. He would've seen sense eventually, as they all did. Sophie hadn't liked her from the first time she'd set eyes on her, and she had no idea why people put up with her shit. Tell a lie — she knew exactly why the guys did. A guaranteed shag on tap meant a lot of other things could be easily overlooked.

'Don't you ever worry that one of us might be next?' Charlie said, his voice almost a whisper.

Alex laughed. 'What, next to top ourselves? Nah, I'll be alright mate. You fill your boots if you fancy it, though.'

This time, Sophie decided to keep quiet. The boys in the group had always had a relationship based on what they called 'banter', but which Sophie had long suspected was deeper than that. Tom and Guy had been more lighthearted and jovial in their digs, but Charlie and Alex had always seemed to mean it. Now Tom and Guy were gone, so was any doubt in her mind as to the sheer cruelty of Charlie and her husband.

She'd long known Alex had an angry side, but he'd changed since Tom died, and even more since Guy. They might not have seen each other as often as they used to, but when they did it was like they'd never been apart. That's why she'd found it so hard to understand Alex's reaction to it all. It was as if he'd just dismissed that all the moment they died, as if it didn't matter anymore.

'I don't want anyone else dying,' Megan said, so quietly that she almost went unheard.

Sophie moved towards her. 'Hey, come on. No-one else is going to die.'

'You don't know that,' Charlie said, receiving dirty looks

from Sophie and Alex. 'What? We didn't know Tom or Guy were going to die either, did we?'

Sophie had hoped Charlie Ford might slink off after Tom's death. The only reason he'd been included as part of the group was because he was Tom's cousin. But now it seemed he was bedding himself in for the long haul.

'Did you mean what you said a moment ago?' Megan asked, turning to Charlie. 'About one of us being next.'

Charlie shrugged. 'Well we don't know, do we? The cops think Tom was killed. They think someone murdered him.'

'But why? Why would someone do that?'

'Maybe Guy killed him then topped himself,' Alex said.

Sophie was aghast. 'Alex!'

'What? It's a theory. If Tom *was* murdered, we need to damn well hope Guy was his killer.'

'Hope? Why on earth would we want to hope that?'

Alex swallowed and looked at her. 'Because otherwise, the killer's still out there. There's a good chance he killed Guy, too. And there's a very good chance he isn't finished yet.'

25

By the time Caroline got home, her head was throbbing. She'd started to feel her energy levels dropping earlier, and knew she was in for a rough couple of days. Still, she'd deal with it the best she could. Her brain, though, was far from tired. Her mind was rarely in sync with her body, it seemed. If she was tired, her mind was active. When she felt brain-dead, her physical energy kept her awake.

She sat on the sofa after dinner and flicked through a couple of local magazines Mark had picked up on his journeys. He had a habit of mindlessly grabbing whatever he could find that focused on the Rutland area, from local business glossies to country living magazines and parish information leaflets. He'd always been someone who was keen to learn as much as he could about everything he could, and it was that infectious enthusiasm which had attracted her to him in the first place.

She was starting to feel her brain winding down and

weighing up whether to go to bed when her phone rang. It was Dexter.

'Dex, what's up?' she said, hoping to every god that he wasn't ringing to tell her they'd found another suicide.

'Not much, you?'

'No, I'm fine.'

'Cool. Cool.'

'Why are you ringing me then, Dex?'

'Oh. Yeah. I've been doing some research. I know, I know, I do surprise you. But listen, I've been looking at patterns of suicides. We don't get many in Rutland. Hardly surprising, perhaps, but there we go. Hangings are even rarer. But Tom Medland and Guy Sherman aren't alone. There've actually been three in the past couple of years. The other one was actually just a few weeks before I joined.'

Caroline's jaw tensed. 'Go on.'

'Never any suspicious circumstances in that one, though. Man of a similar age, but not quite the same. Two years younger. Left a note. Expressed suicidal tendencies for a while. Two previous attempts.'

'So not really the same thing at all, is it?'

'No, but what if he was the first and Tom Medland and Guy Sherman killed themselves because of it? What if he started the suicide cult?'

Caroline sighed and rubbed her head. 'Dex, I think we should both get some sleep.'

Dexter was silent for a moment. 'You still think Tom Medland was murdered, don't you?' he said, eventually.

'Honestly? I don't know. I'm almost certain Tom Medland and Guy Sherman's deaths are linked somehow. It's too convenient otherwise. Same age, same school. We'll get there, Dex. We will.'

'Alright,' Dexter said eventually. 'Alright. I just... There's something that worries me.'

'What's that?' she asked. She heard Dexter swallow at the other end of the phone.

'What if they're not the last to die?'

26

Charlie Ford lit his joint and watched as Megan climbed out of the bed, admiring her body as she put her clothes back on.

'At least open a window,' she said, waving her arm about and curling up her nose as if he'd just sparked up a dog turd.

'What's the problem? Worried someone might smell something on you? Don't think it's a bit of weed you want to be worried about, love. You could've at least waited until he was cold.'

'Just open a fucking window, alright?'

Charlie looked at her for a moment, then got up and pushed open the top pane of glass, the arm creaking and squeaking as he pulled it out to prop the window open. 'Not many women of your age who can still look like that in tight jeans.'

Megan turned to look at him. 'Why do I get the feeling there's some sort of dig hidden in there somewhere?'

'I dunno,' Charlie said, shrugging. 'Low self-esteem, maybe?'

'Fuck off.'

'What, from my own house?'

'It isn't yours and you know it. You don't have anything.'

'I just had you.'

'Like I said. Fuck off.'

Charlie laughed. 'Not what you were saying five minutes ago. Besides, have a little courtesy. I've waited nearly twenty years for this moment.'

'You're sick. Twenty years ago, I was twelve.'

'I said nearly twenty years. You were probably fifteen. Not that that ever stopped you.'

'And what would you know?' she said, tying back her hair. 'I never went anywhere near you. Hardly surprising, really. Look at the state of you.'

'Yet... you just did. Mind you, I guess I was probably just next on the list. You went through everyone else at least once. Even all the nerdy kids. Is it true you noshed off Simon Butler behind the science block? Maybe it was just my turn, eh?'

Megan strode towards Charlie and slapped him across the face, taking him by surprise. Charlie stood for a moment, looking at the wall, feeling the ache starting to develop in his jaw. Then he slowly nodded. 'Like I say. Once a slapper, always a slapper.'

27

It took all the strength Caroline had to haul herself into a sitting position, her muscles tight and aching as she stretched her legs out in front of her on the bed. She hated waking up feeling like this, but on the plus side, at least she was waking up. Without the chemotherapy, that might not have been a daily certainty.

She'd taken to sleeping with a bandana on, unable to face finding clumps of hair on her pillow each morning. Her consultant had warned her the side effects would be more severe with the new course of chemotherapy, and he'd been right. Her previous treatment had felt more concentrated. She hadn't suffered hair loss, and most of her side effects had been digestive, apart from a cycle of general lethargy. Both had been easy enough to hide, but now she stood no chance of that.

In a way, she felt thankful her hand had been forced. There was no way to cover the destruction the chemotherapy was causing to her body — and particularly, she hoped, the tumour on her ovary. She knew her hat would soon have to be swapped for — or complemented by — a wig. Another part of her felt boxed in by that. She'd been given no real option. No choice, other than to go hell-for-leather and wear the hairless look with absolute pride. For Caroline, though, being able to get on with things without having to answer questions or suffer other people's pity and good wishes was paramount in her mind.

She didn't do fuss. She never had. She had been brought up to get on with things and hope for the best. She was often accused of burying her head in the sand, but that wasn't the case. She worried about things as much as the next person, if not more, but she saw no reason to complain or brood over them. She was far more of a fan of moving forward.

Mark appeared in the doorway and put a hot mug of coffee down on the beside table.

'How you feeling?'

'Put it this way. If I get any more mornings where I wake up more exhausted than when I went to bed, I shan't bother. I'm starting to wonder if this "sleep" thing might just be a big con.'

'It's a good thing,' Mark said, sitting on the bed next to her, kissing her bandana-covered head. 'It means your body's spending all its energy fighting the disease overnight. They're Caroline Spencer cells, don't forget. They're tough as nails.'

Caroline smiled. Mark often referred to her using her maiden name when he was complimenting her. To her, it felt romantic, as if he was reminding her of the woman he fell in love with. 'I'm more than happy being a Hills,' she said.

'And I'm more than happy that you are one, but spending

too much time with us Hillses will only make you soppy as custard. And trust me, that tough core's all Spencer.'

Caroline laughed. 'You just want the wrinkled exterior with all the bits falling off to be Hills, yeah?'

'Fits the bill perfectly,' Mark replied, smiling and kissing her again.

'Is that the telly?' she said, noticing the faint sound of canned laughter coming from downstairs.

'Yeah. I know, I know. No TV before school. But you looked so knackered, I didn't want the boys running around or coming up and disturbing you.'

'You mean you didn't want them seeing me looking like shit,' she replied, smiling.

'I think you look wonderful as you are. Besides, didn't we just agree the manky bits were all Hills? For that reason alone, I must take full responsibility,' Mark said, placing his hand on his chest with mock humility.

Caroline smiled again. And in that moment, she realised energy didn't just come from her own body.

28

Caroline arrived at work hoping it would be a good day. She needed it to be. She was in an hour or two later than normal, having had a hospital appointment first thing. They'd done a scan to see if the heavier chemotherapy had been working, and told her she should have results within a week or so. Although she felt positive on that front, her frustrations with work were growing exponentially.

With pressure from up above, and Derek Arnold and EMSOU breathing down her neck, she was desperate for the breakthrough which would let her show her superiors she was making good progress. She was thankful nothing had got into the media, other than brief mentions that two men had been found dead. The link had not yet been publicly made by anyone, but she knew it was only a matter of time.

At that point, the pressure would really be on. They were still reeling from two recent murders, which had rocked the county and its residents. Although that case had been solved, it wasn't without unnecessary bloodshed, public unease and a growing discomfort with the actions of the local police.

Chief Superintendent Derek Arnold could've thrown her under the bus. She had been the Senior Investigating Officer in charge of that case. It had been her decision not to refer it up to the East Midlands Special Operations Unit. She'd chosen to break with protocol on that, leaving herself solely responsible. It was she who'd been put on gardening leave, then chosen to access confidential police information and apprehend the killer in his own home. But still, Arnold had protected her.

She couldn't quite work the man out. He'd made a point of putting the pressure on her a number of times, suggesting the case be passed to EMSOU, berating her for not making progress, removing her from the case when the second murder occurred. Why had he not pounced on it with both paws and had her transferred, demoted or sacked altogether?

On the contrary, he'd visited her at home following the conclusion of Operation Forelock and offered her his full support. It would be fair to say her self-esteem had been knocked by what had happened during Operation Forelock, and she knew she probably wasn't looking at things with a clear head. After all, she was the one who'd identified the killer. She was the one who'd apprehended him and stopped him at the last minute from going to the grave an innocent man. She wondered if perhaps she should take more credit for that than she'd allowed herself so far.

It was a subject that had come up with Rachel, her therapist, in one of their first sessions. The topic of work had, perhaps inevitably, come up very quickly, and it had been clear that Operation Forelock had taken a big toll on Caroline's health. One thing was for certain: she didn't want Operation Utopia to go the same way.

A knock at the door startled her, and she jumped a little before steeling her nerves.

'Come in.'

It was Sara Henshaw. 'Sorry to disturb you. But I think we might have a result on the car that was used to transport Tom Medland's body to Manton. I've been running through the list of owners of that particular model, and one name jumped out at me.'

'Go on,' Caroline said, leaning forward.

'Tom's girlfriend. Megan Wilkes.'

29

Megan loved her job. It gave her a sense of freedom she wouldn't get anywhere else, and it gave her a reason and incentive to stay fit and healthy. After all, she wouldn't get many clients as a personal trainer and yoga instructor if she waddled into the room with a McDonald's bag under her arm.

She'd noticed the police officers at the back of the room a few minutes from the end of the yoga class she was teaching. They'd had the good grace not to come in uniform or to disturb the class, but they still stood out like a sore thumb.

Within minutes, she was sitting in the back of their car, en route to Oakham Police Station.

MEGAN WAS CLEARLY unhappy to be in the interview room, but it seemed to Caroline this was more a feeling of irritation at having had her day disrupted and her image tarnished than any real shock and disbelief that she was being interviewed under caution in relation to her boyfriend's murder.

Once the interview had begun, Caroline got straight into it.

'Can you describe your relationship with Thomas Medland for me, please?'

Megan took a deep breath, then sighed heavily. 'He was my life partner. We'd not been together all that long, but we'd known each other for years.'

'How did you get together?'

'Tom was married for a while, but he got divorced recently. He got treated like shit by her. Lost pretty much everything. We got chatting a bit more, then gradually got closer and ended up as a couple.'

'Were you happy?'

'Very,' Megan replied, pointedly.

'And you'd known Thomas for how long?'

'I'd known *Tom* since school.'

'Secondary school?'

'Yeah.'

'So you were, what, eleven or so?'

'Probably, yeah.'

'Were you friends immediately?'

'Christ, I dunno. Maybe? I don't remember the exact date we signed the Great Friendship Treaty, if that's what you mean.'

'Alright. And fast-forwarding a lot further, did you and Tom live together?'

'No, Tom was living with his parents.'

'And you?'

'I've got a flat.'

'Were you never tempted to move him in with you? You called him your life partner earlier.'

'So? Doesn't mean we have to live together straight away, does it? Anyway, it's a small flat. And I like my space sometimes.'

Caroline nodded. 'Alright. So you've got a flat. What about a car?'

'Yeah, obviously I've got a car.'

'What make and model?'

'A Vauxhall Corsa.'

'Oooh, I like those. New model?'

'Previous one. Why?'

'Do you ever drive it out to Manton?'

Megan looked at Caroline, then at Dexter. 'Why Manton? That's where Tom's body was found.'

'I know. And we believe it was taken there in a Vauxhall Corsa. A dark one. What colour's yours?'

Megan swallowed. 'Black.'

'Pretty dark, then. Where were you between ten o'clock on the evening of the thirteenth and six o'clock on the morning of the fourteenth, Megan?'

'That's the night Tom died.'

'I'm aware of that. Can you answer the question, please?'

Megan thought for a moment before speaking. 'I was at home. It was overnight. Where else would I be?'

'That's what I'm asking. Does your car have a tracker?' Caroline asked, already knowing the answer but wanting to crank up the pressure on Megan.

'No.'

'I see. Do you have CCTV at home?'

'No.'

Caroline nodded as she pretended to jot a few words down on her notepad. 'And what about witnesses? Do you have an alibi who can corroborate your statement that you were at home?'

'I... I live on my own. I told you,' Megan said.

'So, in other words, no alibi either?'

Megan looked at the table and dropped her head, then lifted it slowly before speaking again.

'Well... Look. There is someone. Someone was with me. But if I tell you who, you have to promise me you'll never tell a soul.'

30

He was starting to feel very unhappy with the way things had been going recently. He'd made one or two mistakes — who hadn't? — but now he was beginning to feel everything unraveling around him. He didn't think he was a bad person. Not at heart. But sometimes one lie, one mistruth, led you down a road from which there was no return. He'd got so tangled up in lies and misdirection, he barely knew himself what the truth was anymore.

The plan had been to move away. London looked most promising, if he was able to get a job there. And he'd need a high-paying one to live in London. Plenty of jobs came up in Cambridge, but that was no good. Not far enough. It wouldn't give them a reason to up sticks and move. There was a lot of money in advertising if you found the right employer. And he'd certainly found the right employer. He'd been on the verge of accepting a job in London — although the salary wouldn't allow them to buy a place any more central than

Croydon at best — when he was headhunted by Charnley & Walker. His first instinct had been to turn the job down. Charnley & Walker were based in Stamford, where they lived, and he was keen to move away. Very keen. But when he told them he was thinking of accepting a job in London, they doubled the salary they were offering. Eighty-five grand a year! And he'd be an Account Director, not just an Account Manager. Even in London, he'd be lucky to earn sixty. It'd been a no-brainer: take the Charnley & Walker job, get that position and salary on his CV then start looking for the *really* big payday in London. He'd be a partner at a big London advertising agency within two years — he knew it. He could feel it in his bones.

Staying in the area had its risks, though. Risks that could be more easily overlooked for eighty-five grand a year, but risks that were nonetheless still there. It wouldn't be long before tongues started wagging and people started probing, and he had far too much to lose to risk that. But, at the end of the day, when all was said and done, money talked.

He was a big fan of clichés. In many ways, his life had been one big one. But he found there was often a perfectly good cliché for almost every situation. Advertising execs loved them, and for good reason. Why invent new words and phrases when everyone knows what you mean by 'Never look a gift-horse in the mouth'? The idea that everything needed to be 'fresh' or 'original' made him squirm. It was horseshit, and everyone in advertising knew it. What worked was familiarity. Relevance. Give them comfort, something they know and love. But things had been getting a little too familiar and comfortable for him recently. And he was going to have to do something about it.

The ringing of the doorbell jolted him from his reverie, and he walked downstairs to answer the door.

'Alex Lawson?'

'Yes,' he replied.

'Detective Inspector Caroline Hills. This is my colleague, Detective Sergeant Dexter Antoine. We'd like to have a little chat, is that okay?'

Alex tensed his jaw. 'Uh, yeah. Sure. Come in.'

CAROLINE SMILED as Alex stepped aside to let them in. The house was, like most houses in Stamford, built in traditional sandstone, and the interior was fresh and clean.

'Sophie's not in,' he said, gesturing to an empty space in the hall. 'She's at work. Should I call her?'

'No need,' Caroline replied. 'Day off yourself?'

'I work from home on Fridays.'

'Nice work if you can get it.'

'Only saves me a three minute drive, to be honest. It's one of these new initiatives the bosses came up with to make the company more "modern". Nothing at all to do with the fact they like to play golf on Fridays, of course.'

Caroline smiled. 'No, I'm sure that's just a huge coincidence. Can we go and sit down?' she asked, pointing through into the living room.

'Oh right. Yeah, course. Sorry.'

Although Caroline was a fan of hard flooring, she was yet to be convinced that anything other than a thick pile carpet should be on a living room floor. The Lawsons had gone for hard flooring and a large rug, which did nothing to soak up the cold echos that bounced around the room, making it sound more like a prison cell than a comfortable, cosy living room.

'We just wanted to ask you a few questions, if that's okay. We understand you were a friend of Tom Medland, is that right?'

'Yeah. Yeah, I guess so.'

'You guess so?' Dexter asked.

'Well, I mean, we knew each other. Went to school together. Didn't see each other as often as we used to, though.'

'What about his girlfriend, Megan?' Caroline asked.

'What about her?'

'Do you know her well?'

Alex shrugged. 'Known her a while. She comes and goes.'

'Do you see her often?'

'Not really, no.'

'When was the last time you saw her?'

Alex looked towards the window and sighed. 'Christ, I've no idea. I don't have a specific date, if that's what you mean.'

'Okay,' Caroline said, nodding and looking down at her notepad. 'And Guy Sherman was a friend of yours too, wasn't he?'

'Well, yeah. Again, he's someone I knew from school, and saw maybe a few times a year.'

'Were you close at school?' Dexter asked.

'Closer. We all were. Everyone drifts apart as they get

older. Close enough to be upset that they're dead, if that's what you mean.'

'And when did you last see Guy?' Caroline asked.

'Now that one's a bit easier. I saw him maybe a week or two ago, sitting outside The Vaults in Uppingham. He was having a drink with a friend so I didn't hang around, but just a quick "hi, how's it going" sort of thing.'

'How did he seem?'

'Uh, fine. But like I say, I was probably only with him about ten or twenty seconds. He didn't manage to squeeze in a mention of his plans to top himself, if that's what you mean.'

'And Tom? Did he seem okay in himself? No sign that he was thinking of harming himself?'

'No, he seemed fine. But as I said, I hadn't seen him in a while.'

'Not depressed at all?'

'No, quite the opposite. He was always a really happy-go-lucky kind of guy.'

'He hadn't found out you'd been shagging his girlfriend, then?' Caroline looked at Alex and waited for a response, but he looked like a rabbit caught in the headlights. 'I mean, that's where you were on the Sunday night, isn't it? At Megan Wilkes's flat?'

'I... Uh, I don't remember.'

'What did you tell your wife? How did you manage to explain that one away?'

Alex looked at the floor, then held his head in his hands. A few moments later, he spoke.

'She was at her mum's in Bourne. Sophie wasn't at work on Monday, so her and her mum went out for dinner and some drinks on Sunday night because it was her dad's birthday. Would've been, anyway. He died earlier this year.'

'Oh right, I see. So while your wife was commemorating her dead father's birthday, you were out shagging Tom Medland's girlfriend. Why didn't you join them for the meal?'

Alex swallowed. 'I had a load of work to get done on the Sunday, and I was in the office first thing Monday. Plus her mum doesn't really like me.'

'How strange. I wonder why.'

'Look, I don't need your judgement, alright? I know how it looks. I'm not proud.'

'How long's it been going on?' Dexter asked.

Alex sighed. 'Too long. It's been on and off for years. If you've met Megan, and I presume you have because no-one else knew I was there, you'll know what she's like. It's...'

'Convenient?' Caroline asked.

'Complicated.'

'And Sophie doesn't know about this?'

'No, of course she bloody doesn't. And she doesn't need to, either. I'll deal with that myself.'

'I'm sure you will,' Caroline said. 'I'm sure you will.' As far as she was concerned, she had everything she needed. Megan Wilkes's car matched that which was used to dump Tom Medland's body. She and Alex Lawson had been seeing each other behind their respective partners' backs. There was more than enough in terms of motive, means and opportunity. Although the case of Guy Sherman would take more investigation and exploration, she had more than enough reason to bring Lawson in over Tom Medland's death. That way, they could seize assets and evidence which could link him to both men's deaths. 'Alex Lawson,' she said, standing up and gesturing for him to do the same, 'I'm arresting you on suspicion of the murder of Thomas Medland. You do not have to say anything, but it may harm your defence if you do not mention when questioned something which you later rely on in court. Anything you do say may be given in evidence.'

31

Caroline and Dexter had prepared their line of questioning for the official interview and felt confident they could make strong progress. They'd have twenty-four hours to either charge or release him, and Caroline was sure that would be more than enough time — especially now Lawson knew he was on the ropes.

As they left the incident room to head down to the interview suite, Aidan called out to them.

'Boss, hold up. We've got something.'

'What is it, Aidan?' Caroline said, walking over to his desk.

'You asked us to get onto wider CCTV. We managed to track down a guy on Lyndon Road in Manton, who's got cameras on the front of his house. He said he'd had problems with people parking in front of his driveway when they were visiting the pub, so he's got them covering the road, too. We managed to get the footage from him for Sunday night and Monday morning. A fair bit to comb through, but look at this.'

Caroline leaned in and watched the footage on Aidan's screen as he hit the play button. A couple of moments later, he paused the footage.

'See that car?'

'Dark Vauxhall Corsa.'

'Exactly. Now watch.' Aidan unpaused the video again, and the team watched as the car slowed before turning into St Mary's Road, just yards away from the Horse & Jockey pub and Cemetery Lane. 'There's not really anywhere else they could be going,' Aidan said. 'But now have a look at this one. It's from another corner of his house. You get a different angle.' Aidan played the video, and they watched as the same footage played again from another viewpoint. As the car came into shot, he paused the playback. 'Okay, so at this point we've got a decent view of the back of the car. Numberplate, the lot.'

'The plate's just a massive white blob, though,' Caroline said.

'At the moment it is. Infrared camera, see? The light above the plate has interfered with it. So what I did is take that screen-grab and run it through here,' he said, switching to an image editing program Caroline didn't recognise, 'and adjust the lighting levels. If we bring the contrast right down over the plate...'

As Aidan spoke, the registration number of the car became visible.

'Jesus Christ. You learn something new every day,' Caroline said. 'Have we done a lookup on that registration?'

'We have,' Aidan replied. 'Vehicle licensing comes back as being registered to a Miss Megan Wilkes.'

Caroline felt the hairs stand up on the back of her neck as

she and Dexter realised the enormity of the evidence in front of them. Megan Wilkes's car, heading straight to the dump site of Tom Medland's body, in the early hours of Monday morning. In that moment, she felt more certain than ever that they had their killer.

32

Alex Lawson didn't look at all comfortable sitting in the police interview suite, but then again not many people did. He'd opted for the services of the duty solicitor, something which was either smart or foolish, depending on your line of defence and the lawyer that happened to be on duty at the time.

Megan Wilkes's car had been seized and was currently being swabbed by forensics for any trace that Tom Medland's body had been transported in it. If the results came back positive, they'd have solid grounds to charge Alex and Megan with Tom's murder.

Caroline decided they should get the interview with Alex Lawson started. Meanwhile, Sara and Aidan would interview Megan to see what she had to say for herself.

Caroline kicked off the interview in the usual way, then detailed what Alex had told them at his house.

'You stated that you'd been in an on-off sexual relationship with Megan Wilkes, recent girlfriend of the deceased, Thomas Medland, for a number of years. You also stated that on the night of Sunday the thirteenth of September, you stayed at Miss Wilkes's flat and returned home on the morning of Monday, the fourteenth of September. Is that correct?'

Alex glanced at his solicitor. Caroline knew the brief would, no doubt, have advised him to reply with 'no comment' to that, as it would only be admissible evidence when said under police caution. To her surprise, Alex then looked down at the table, then up at her.

'How much of this will get back to Sophie?' he said.

'Well, we can look at it two ways. If you're innocent and we don't charge you, everything remains confidential and you're free to tell her as much or as little as you want. Only your conscience can dictate that. If there's enough evidence to bring you to court, or if you're guilty, then it'd almost certainly come out in the courtroom. But at that point, I don't think admitting to having a bit on the side is going to be your biggest problem.'

Alex seemed to think about this for a few moments, then slowly nodded. 'Okay. Yes. That's all correct.'

Caroline could see his solicitor squirming beside him as he raised an eyebrow and jotted down a few notes on the papers in front of him.

'Good. Thank you,' Caroline said. 'Can you tell me a little more about what happened that night? What did you do?'

'What, do you want a diagram?'

'That's very kind, but I've got two children. I can work that bit out. Just a brief overview will be fine.'

'We watched a bit of TV, then we had sex.'

'Quite the romantic evening. And you slept there?'

'Yes.'

'In the same bed?'

'Well it would've been a bit weird if I'd shaken her hand, said "thanks very much" and gone to sleep in the spare room, wouldn't it?'

'Is that a yes?'

Alex rolled his eyes. 'Yes.'

'And did you stay there all night?'

'No, I got up in the middle of the night to pop to the shop. Yes, I stayed there all night.'

'And what time did you leave?'

Alex leaned back and took a deep breath. 'I dunno, about eight I think? I had to get to work.'

'Very responsible. Tell me, Alex. What car does Megan drive?'

'Uh, a Corsa I think. Yeah. Black one.'

'A bit like this one?' Caroline said, passing a print-out of the CCTV imagery to him.

'Well, yeah, that's a Corsa. Not a great picture, though.'

'Do you know her car registration number?'

Alex laughed. 'No. Obviously not. I'm not even sure of my own.'

'Do you think you might recognise it if you saw it?'

'I doubt it.'

'And what if I told you a dark Vauxhall Corsa was seen in the early hours of Monday morning, heading for the location where Tom Medland's body was found a few hours later, and that this particular car is registered to Megan Wilkes, the girl-friend of Tom Medland and the woman you'd been sleeping with?'

Alex swallowed. His solicitor leaned over and whispered something in his ear.

'No comment,' Alex said.

Caroline smiled. It had only been a matter of time. 'You should know we've arrested Megan too, Alex. We've put the same evidence to her. Only difference is, she's talking.'

It was a cleverly worded sentence from Caroline. It was designed to imply that Megan had opened up and told them the whole truth, and that Alex would be digging himself into a deeper hole if he didn't tell them what had happened that night. The transcripts in court, however, would be more ambiguous. The words 'she's talking' didn't explicitly state Megan had made any admissions. Caroline would simply say she was referring to the fact that Megan hadn't been no-commenting her way through her interview. The truth was, Caroline had no idea what Megan was doing. She'd left Aidan and Sara to handle her initial interview while she and Dexter closed ranks on Alex Lawson.

'What's she said?' Alex asked, clearly rattled by Caroline's ruse.

'She's told us the truth as she sees it. Now it's time for you to have your say.'

'I haven't got anything to say.'

'Alright,' Caroline said, nodding slowly. 'And what about Guy Sherman?'

'What about him?'

'Did you know him well?'

'Pretty well, yeah. I went to school with him. Saw him socially every now and then.'

'He died in very similar circumstances to Tom, didn't he? What do you make of that?'

Alex's solicitor leaned over and whispered in his ear again, this time for a few seconds longer.

'I've got no further comment,' Alex said. 'I'd like to have some time to speak with my solicitor in private.'

33

By the time Caroline and Dexter got back to the incident room, Sara and Aidan were already back at their desks.

'How'd it go?' Sara asked.

Caroline took a deep breath and sighed. 'About as well as could be expected. He confirmed what he'd admitted when we spoke to him at his house. We turned the pressure up a bit, showed him the CCTV of the car and mentioned it was registered to Megan. Solicitor whispered in his ear and suddenly it was No Comment City. How about you?'

'Much the same. She says Alex came over to hers around seven o'clock on Sunday night and left about eight o'clock on Monday morning. She says neither of them left her flat at any point.'

Caroline nodded. 'Find out who owns the block of flats. Megan said there isn't any CCTV, but there is some that covers the car park. We've got someone reviewing the footage, so we'll be able to see if they did leave. Does her car have a tracker?'

Sara shook her head. 'Not on that model, no. Not as standard. Both their mobile phones are showing as having stayed in the same location overnight, too. Megan's flat. Alex's starts moving at four minutes past eight on Monday morning. Megan's on the move just after ten. She received a call from Tom's mother, Lorraine Medland, a couple of minutes earlier.'

'Where'd she go?'

'To her parents' place in Whissendine.'

'That's the opposite direction from Manton,' Caroline said.

'I know. She said she didn't want to see the body. Didn't want to visit him in the mortuary. Just wanted to be with her parents.'

Caroline thought about this for a few moments. Grief affected different people in different ways, but something about this felt odd to her. 'Did she drive?'

'So she says. No ANPR hits, but phone triangulation shows her heading straight out through Langham and into Whissendine. Her parents live right on the northern edge of the village. She came home mid-afternoon.'

'Strange. If she wanted to be with them at a time of grief, why didn't she stay?'

'They had an argument, apparently.'

Caroline raised an eyebrow.

'I know,' Sara said. 'But believe me, after spending time in an interview room with her, I can well believe it. We have a bit of a problem, though.'

'Go on.'

'We got lucky with forensics on the car. Ish.'

'Ish?'

'Well, Megan's car was impounded as soon as she was arrested and they got straight to work on a DNA sweep. They found some traces of blood in the boot, but it'll be a day or two before they can tell us if it's Tom's blood. Tom's fingerprints were found inside the car, indicating he'd been a passenger fairly recently. At least since the car was last cleaned. Also a few on the driver's side, but not so many. It's impossible to say when they were deposited, though.'

'Christ. Okay. Let's think this through,' Caroline said. 'The prints match. Ergo, Tom — at some point — sat in the passenger seat of Megan's car. As you say, not unusual, but easy enough to determine in itself. Worst case scenario, the blood isn't his. What's to say Megan didn't drive him to Manton, still alive and well, then kill him there? Maybe Alex was with them, or met them there. He'd have to have arrived on foot, though, from the other end.'

'Or,' Aidan said, raising his hand, 'what if we're looking at this from the wrong angle? The prints showed he'd been in the driver's seat too, right?'

'Yeah. Far fewer, but they were there,' Sara said.

'So it's possible he drove himself to Manton. What if he was the driver we saw on the CCTV footage?'

Caroline scratched her head. 'What, you think he drove himself to his own murder?'

'No, his own suicide. Let's roll back. What if the damage to the undergrowth and vegetation *was* coincidental or caused by something else? What if it *was* suicide?'

'Then who drove his car away? And how did the blood get in the boot?'

'Well, I hadn't quite got that far,' Aidan said, chided.

'Maybe someone else was in on it,' Dexter offered. 'Could still be Alex. Maybe Tom was cut up after his divorce, had a few drinks perhaps, found out about him and Megan, and Alex convinced him this was a painless way out.'

'That's another point,' Caroline said. 'Tom had been drinking for hours with his cousin, Charlie Ford. How's he meant to have driven himself to Manton and lobbed himself off a railway bridge? And where did the car come from? He either managed to somehow get to her place while blind drunk and pick it up, or someone else brought it over to him, got out and let him drive, even though he was plastered. It doesn't add up.'

'It's a theory,' Aidan said, shrugging.

'Yep, it's possible,' Caroline replied, hoping she hadn't offended him. 'But I don't think it's strong enough to go to the CPS with. I think we've got a much better case if our theory is that Megan and Alex drove Tom down Cemetery Lane. Maybe Tom found out about them. Alex had the most to lose. What if Tom threatened to tell Sophie what had been going on? Alex snaps and strangles him. They panic, drive him to Manton, and carry his body down the embankment, before tying the rope around his neck and hurling him off, leaving him hanging in the opening of the tunnel. It'd be so much easier with two people. Means, motive, opportunity. They left their phones at home, knowing we'd be able to trace them otherwise. They were smart enough to avoid main roads, but didn't realise there'd be a CCTV camera on the side of the Horse and Jockey pub. That was their downfall. Any thoughts?'

'Only a worry that it's not strong enough,' Dexter said. 'If we had forensic evidence proving Alex and Megan had been at Manton, we'd be solid. Mud on their shoes could be matched up, perhaps something under their fingernails.'

'They were arrested days after the murder,' Caroline said, shaking her head. 'Fingernail swabs will be next to useless. We've no way of knowing what clothing or footwear they wore, either. Their houses have been searched, but nothing suspicious has been flagged up so far.'

'Phone records, then?' Dexter offered. 'If we can prove an ongoing relationship between Alex and Megan, we're in with a far better shout.'

'They've both admitted the ongoing relationship. There's no evidence of any planning on their phone records, so that backs up the spur-of-the-moment thing. Just a few flirty and dirty messages on — what was it, Aidan? Instagram?'

'Telegram. An encrypted messaging app.'

'That's the one. If they had the foresight to try to hide their route and leave their phones at home, it's highly unlikely they'd have planned it all using their phones. It's the sort of thing that will've been done in person.'

'But there's no evidence of them luring Tom either, is there? On their phones, I mean.'

'No. But again, that'd leave a trace. And anyway, if they were planning to get rid of someone so they could be together, Sophie would be the obvious choice.'

'Maybe,' Dexter replied. 'But the only thing that troubles me there is that Megan's car doesn't pop up on ANPR or CCTV anywhere in Oakham that night.'

'Okay. Well, maybe she was just lucky. It's all we've got,' Caroline said.

If she was honest with herself, she knew there was an element of grasping at straws. However, straws were all she had. She needed to show her superiors she was making strong progress.

'And what about Guy Sherman?' Sara asked. 'We can't tie anyone to his death.'

Caroline shrugged. 'Maybe that *was* suicide. Could be completely unconnected. Occam's Razor, Sara. The simplest explanation is usually the right one. If it doesn't look like there's a connection between the two, there's probably no connection between the two. Guy showed no sign of having put up a struggle. There were some rope fibres under his fingernails, but that's not unusual in suicidal hangings. It's instinctive, especially if they haven't worked out the proper drop measurements.'

'So that's what we're going with?' Dexter asked. 'Alex and Megan killed Tom, whether premeditated or not, and Guy Sherman killed himself in a completely unrelated incident.'

Caroline swallowed. 'There's every chance Tom's death contributed to his depression or reasons for wanting to end his own life. That'd be perfectly reasonable to suggest. Like you said a couple of days ago, look at that town in Wales.'

'Bridgend.'

'Exactly. Butterfly effect.'

There were a few moments' silence as Caroline thought. The pressure from her superiors, and the desire to see closure on this case would have been enough on its own, but the more she thought about it, the more she mulled over the circumstances, relationships and dynamics in this case, the more certain she was in her theory. There was no evidence to the contrary, and plenty to support it. Any missing certainty could easily be explained by Alex and Megan having planned Tom's murder carefully. It happened, from time to time. But this time, she was sure, they hadn't quite been careful enough.

'Okay. I've made a decision,' she said, taking a deep breath and addressing the team. 'I'm going to Chief Superintendent Arnold. I'm going to request an extension to their custody clocks.'

There was a knock at the door, and PC Joe Lloyd popped his head round. 'Sorry,' he said. 'Quick update on that CCTV you asked me to look over. Her car's parked up in its space all night.'

'All night?' Caroline asked.

'Yep. Doesn't budge an inch.'

34

Caroline was shell-shocked. She'd put it all on black, and the winning number couldn't have been more red. There wasn't enough evidence to charge, and the CCTV revelation proved it hadn't been Megan's car that was used to transport Tom's body. That alone would mean she'd be unlikely to get an extension on the custody clocks.

They could prove a car bearing Megan Wilkes's registration plates had headed in the general direction of Cemetery Lane, and they could prove Tom Medland had, at some point, driven and been a passenger in his girlfriend's car. But they now knew those two cars were not one and the same.

She couldn't help but feel slightly sick at the sight of Alex Lawson's smug face as she and Dexter walked past the custody desk.

'What a waste of bloody time that was,' he called over his shoulder.

Caroline knew she shouldn't react. The right thing to do

was to walk on, walk away. But even as she was telling herself this, she found herself turning round and facing him.

'And what is it about an investigation into the deaths of two of your friends which you think is a "waste of time" exactly?' she asked.

'Arresting people and bringing them in without any evidence. All that time, you could've been out finding who actually did this, couldn't you? Rather than wasting your time on us.'

It was far from the first time Caroline had heard this line, and it usually never even registered with her. But this time it felt like a personal attack — and one she wasn't able to let go.

'And what do you know about policing and murder investigations?'

Dexter put a hand on her forearm. 'Guv.'

Alex stepped forward. 'I know enough to tell you you've made a huge mistake. Crazy bringing us in. Absolutely stupid. Why us, eh? We're not the ones you want. Think about it. It's obvious who's done this. It's obvious who's set us up.'

'Who?' Caroline asked.

Alex answered with a sneer. 'Charlie Ford.'

35

The atmosphere in the Lawson household was frosty that evening, and Alex felt thankful his wife didn't know about the Megan situation, too. Far from merely frosty, the release of that bombshell would send temperatures plummeting to subzero levels.

'Is that what you actually said?' Sophie asked, looking at her husband in disbelief. 'You told them Charlie did it?'

'No, I told them he's the one they want to be harassing and interviewing, not me. The guy's got a criminal record longer than my arm, for Christ's sake. Why the hell did they come after me instead?'

'Good question,' Sophie replied, her voice a little quieter. 'Did they tell you why?'

Alex felt momentarily floored. 'Oh, some bullshit about a witness saying they'd spotted someone who looked a bit like me near the scene.'

'A bit like you?'

'Yeah. Usual vague description. Short dark hair, medium height. Could've been anyone.'

'So why you?'

'I dunno, do I? Because I knew them both, probably. Like I say, could've been anyone.'

'But not Charlie.'

'What do you mean?'

'He's got long hair.'

'Yeah, well, he might've had it tied up or under a hat or something. Maybe this witness saw him from a distance. It was dark, anyway.'

'How do you know?'

'Because it was the middle of the bloody night! Christ, Soph. What is this? I've had enough interrogation for one day, I can tell you that.'

Sophie blinked a few times, then thought for a moment. 'So they think it's definitely one of us, then?'

'How do you mean?'

'You said the police arrested you because you fitted the description and because you knew Tom and Guy.'

Alex sighed. 'Yeah, well it makes sense, doesn't it? It's the only connection.'

'Did they say Guy was definitely murdered?'

Alex shook his head. 'They hardly mentioned him at all. But what are the odds? It's too suspicious, Soph.'

Sophie looked at her husband for a couple of moments. Something wasn't quite right. 'Why are you suddenly so sure they're connected?' she asked.

'I dunno. I just do. Think about it — Charlie was the last

one to see Tom alive, right? And we know what he's like. He's a scumbag. Plus he hated Guy.'

'Charlie hates everyone,' Sophie said. 'Besides, if it was all that obvious, why didn't they arrest him?'

'They spoke to him right at the start.'

'Yeah, but they didn't arrest him, did they? They arrested you, though.'

'What are you trying to say?' Alex said, rounding on her.

'Come on, Alex. It's apparently so obvious Charlie's guilty, but they've arrested you instead of him? What have they got on you?'

'Nothing. They've got nothing on me. It's Charlie Ford. The guy's a scumbag.'

'Well the police must think you're even worse. What have you been up to, Alex?'

Before Sophie could wait for a reply, the breath was knocked from her as her back slammed into the wall, her husband pinning her against it with his hand around her throat.

She looked into his eyes, panic flooding her as he bared his teeth, white spittle forming around the corners of his mouth. She thought he was about to speak, but he didn't. He growled, let go and walked out of the house.

36

In the short time she'd been seeing Rachel for therapy sessions, Caroline already had a lot to thank her for. The thing that appealed most, though, was her flexibility. Whereas many of Rachel's clients were able to commit to the same day and time each week, that was a luxury Caroline didn't have.

She'd thought she'd have to cancel the early evening session she'd arranged, especially after bringing Alex Lawson and Megan Wilkes into custody. But since they'd been released much sooner than she'd hoped, she had been able to keep her appointment.

She'd felt conflicted about it. She was so completely fed up and aggravated by what'd happened that day, there was no way she'd get much out of a session tonight. It'd only infuriate her further. What she wanted was a glass of wine and a long sleep. But part of her wondered if Rachel might be able to help her through those thought processes. After all, that was what she was there for, wasn't it?

Rachel started by asking her how her week had been, and Caroline had told her — with both barrels.

'Has work always made you feel like this?' Rachel asked.

Caroline thought for a moment, then shook her head. 'No. Not really.'

Rachel slowly nodded. 'And why do you think that might be?'

'I don't know. A greater feeling of responsibility, maybe.'

'How do you mean?'

'Well, in London I was part of a much bigger team. Things were more anonymous. It was all office-based, we all had clearly defined roles. There wasn't quite as much pressure. Plus murder was an everyday thing, for better or for worse.'

'And because you're part of a much smaller team up here, you feel a greater responsibility?'

Caroline murmured her agreement, feeling a sudden swell of emotion. After a moment or two, it had passed enough for her to speak again. 'I know people might think I'm this hard-nosed machine that gets things done, but I think deep down that's just a coping mechanism. It's the only way I can deal with things. I have to make sure my emotions are totally separate.'

'Is that a common thing for police officers?'

'It is, but even more so here. It's a different area. Closer. People aren't so anonymous. You feel like you know everyone. When things happen here, they're much bigger. Everything is under the magnifying glass.'

Rachel smiled. 'That's small communities for you.'

'Yeah. Tell me about it.'

'Is it all bad, then? The different way things operate here, I mean.'

Caroline thought for a moment. 'No. No it's not. I think secretly I actually quite like it. It just takes a lot of getting used to.'

'What was it that brought you here? Work?'

'Sort of. But I think it's more of a case of me bringing work here. I've always lived in London, so never really knew anything else. I hadn't really seen how bad things had got and how they were affecting us until I took a step back and looked at it.'

'That's why it's so important sometimes to just stop, breathe and look at the here and now. We're all so worried about things that happened in the past or things that might happen in the future, but we completely ignore what's right here in the present. What was it that made you take a step back?'

'A few things, I think. My eldest, Josh, had been having trouble at school for a while. Bullying. There were a couple of knife crime cases I worked on which got a bit too close to home. It just didn't feel safe anymore. It felt like the world was closing in on us. Then Mark's dad and brother died not far apart. It just... It made us reevaluate life. I think Mark's always been a country boy at heart. He's loving it here. I mean, I am too. I think. I just need a little more time to adjust than he does.'

'Why do you think that might be?'

Caroline felt her heart beating harder. 'I don't know.'

'It's interesting that it sounds like it was your idea to leave London. You mentioned it felt like things were closing in on you. But at the same time, now you're away from there, I get the sense there's something pulling you back.'

Her palms were sweaty now, and she could feel a fluttering in her chest. 'I dunno. Maybe. I don't know.'

'Is there a connection somewhere which has made you feel guilty or ashamed for leaving, do you think?'

'Maybe. Perhaps. I don't know,' Caroline said, a lump rising in her throat.

'You still have family in London, don't you?'

Caroline put her hand in her jacket pocket. 'I'm sorry, that'll be work. My phone. It's vibrating. It'll be important. I need to go,' she said. 'I'll call you.' She stood up and left the room, before making her way back towards her car. There, she threw her phone on the passenger seat beside her, the screen lighting up to show no missed calls and no messages. Caroline put her head in her hands and cried.

37

By the time Caroline got home, she felt numb. Feelings and visions from the past came to her often, but recently they'd got far more vivid. She wondered if the physical distance she'd created by moving to Rutland had forced her mind to focus on it more. It was almost as if creating an emotional *and* physical distance was a snub to what'd happened. Whitewashing it from the tapestry of life. And her mind wouldn't let her do that.

'Good day?' Mark asked as she walked into the house, the familiar smell of his chicken curry wafting through the hallway.

'Yeah. Yeah, not bad,' she replied, keen to avoid having to think about what had really happened.

'I've made a jalfrezi. Not quite as good as Dining Street, but I think I'm getting closer.'

'Thank you. It smells lovely.' And it did. Although the chemotherapy had ruined a lot of smells and tastes for her, she was pleased to discover Mark's chicken curry still had the same mouthwatering appeal. In that moment, as her stomach gave a growl, she realised how long it'd been since she'd last eaten.

They all sat round the table, the first time they'd had a proper family meal in days, and Caroline tried to ignore the clock on the wall that told her the boys were up past their bedtime. She knew Mark had kept them up so they could eat together, and that thought meant more to her than an arbitrary time for sleep. In any case, it was Saturday tomorrow, so they wouldn't have to be up early for school. She wished she could have a lie-in herself, but she'd be in the office at the crack of dawn, pushing on with Operation Utopia.

Caroline noticed Archie looking at her, and smiled. He was looking at her hair again — or lack thereof. The hair loss had accelerated over the past couple of days, but she felt awkward wearing a hat or head covering inside the house.

'It'll grow back, sweetheart,' she said, skewering a piece of chicken with her fork.

'It looks weird,' Archie said.

'You can't say that,' his older brother, Josh replied with a scowl. Caroline had noticed him becoming much more protective over her recently. Part of her wondered whether it was his way of acknowledging the effort she and Mark had made to relocate the family and make them happier.

'It's fine, honestly,' she said, giving them both a smile. 'Trust me, it looks weird to me too. And it feels weird. But I'd far rather have my hair fall out than the alternative. At least this way I'll get better.'

'Will you, though?' Archie asked.

Caroline blinked a couple of times, then forced another

smile. 'Course. Why wouldn't I?' She felt a rising lump in her throat and excused herself, heading upstairs.

She closed the bathroom door behind her and sat on the closed toilet, trying to stifle her sobs so her family wouldn't hear. She was scared, angry, regretful, frustrated. She just wanted everything to be over.

A minute or two later, there was a gentle knock at the door, and Mark stepped inside.

'They're only asking because they care,' he said.

'I know. And that's almost the worst part. I don't want to let them down. I don't want them to think I look weird.'

'You don't,' he said, taking her in his arms. 'You look beautiful. Always.'

'What, even with this?' she said, gesturing towards her head.

'Even with that.'

'I'm tempted to just shave the rest off. It's going to go anyway. No point trying to cling on, hoping it'll stop. It won't, will it?'

Mark shook his head. 'No.'

'Will you help me?'

'Of course I will.'

Caroline opened the bathroom cabinet and took out Mark's beard trimmer — the only hair-cutting tool they owned — and switched it on. She looked into the mirror and handed the trimmer to Mark, watching as he raised it towards her head and nodded. She nodded back.

The vibration felt strange against her head, and she watched as the last remaining wisps of hair tumbled down her face and landed in the white porcelain sink. He was firm, but gentle, catching any last stray bits of hair behind her ears, checking to make sure it was all gone. He moved the trimmer away from her head, and Caroline expected him to switch it off. Instead, he tapped her on the side of the arm to move her to one side, then leaned in towards the mirror before lifting the trimmer to his own head.

Locks of his brown curls dropped into the sink as Caroline's tears fell to the tiled floor, an intense wave of love and warmth flooding through her.

38

Megan Wilkes was starting to feel lonely. If she was honest with herself, she'd always felt lonely, but she'd rarely had any trouble feeling better with a bit of male company. That wasn't possible now, though. With Tom dead and both she and Alex under the watchful gaze of the police, even she was starting to struggle on the companionship front.

Charlie had texted her an hour or two earlier, asking if she was free that evening. She'd been sorely tempted to say yes, but there was no way she was going there after what he said to her last time.

The flat felt empty. It had always been empty, other than her and the odd visitor, but there was something different about it now. It felt more like a permanent emptiness — one which would prove far more difficult to shake off.

She wondered if she'd have to leave and find somewhere else. It was starting to hold too many bad memories for her. At that point, could it truly be considered a home? Megan had always had trouble with the concept of 'home'. Her own parents had kicked her out when she was sixteen, and she'd spent a good couple of years working, sofa surfing and living with a succession of boyfriends until she'd finally scraped together enough money to just about edge a deposit on a flat. Even then it'd been as part of a shared ownership scheme, effectively meaning she part-owned and part-rented, the plan being to gradually buy back the rented portion. It'd been a bit of a joke at first, walking round the flat and wondering which bits she owned and which were rented. She used to tease visitors about where they could stand, or placate spillers of wine on carpets by saying 'Oh, it's okay; I happen to own that bit'.

Part-owning and part-renting meant she'd never had the luxury of being able to save up money, and when this flat came up for sale at a ridiculously affordable price, she'd jumped at the chance. Six months later, she'd personalised it just the way she'd wanted.

She'd often thought about moving away, getting away from it all. But she wasn't sure she was the sort of person who could just up sticks and start again. Rutland was far from being the liveliest place in the world, but it was comfortable. And comfort went a long way with her. It was a sentiment the group seemed to share, too. Guy — good old Guy — had moved away for university and set himself up in Bristol, but had been lured back for work as an architect on some big local tourism projects. Alex and Sophie had planned to relocate for work, too. Alex told Megan it'd all been Sophie's idea, but when he'd been offered silly money by a local company to stick around, Sophie'd had no choice. Now that she thought about it, it didn't make much sense. Why would Sophie have wanted to move further away from her mum and everything she knew? Sophie'd always seemed comfortable where she was. She wondered what reason Alex would have for wanting to move away, but no matter how much she scratched her head, she couldn't think of anything.

She knew the others had never really considered her to be part of the group. Alex had tried to keep her at arm's length, particularly around Sophie, but Megan always got her way. After all, Alex wouldn't want her to 'accidentally' mention they'd been sleeping together on and off for the past few years, would he? Imagine what sort of damage that'd cause! She hadn't ever put it in exactly those words, but she'd made damn sure he didn't exclude her and kept her as part of the group.

Once everyone began to drift apart and see each other less, she'd spotted her chance: Tom. The timing of his marriage break-up and divorce was ideal, and she'd virtually thrown herself at him. She knew she was a rebound case — at least at first — but she was pretty good at making men fall for her.

All she'd ever wanted was company and friends. She'd never felt accepted as a kid, and her parents throwing her out at sixteen had cemented that feeling in her mind. She just hoped they'd be able to keep the group together now. She felt sure they would. After all, Alex had too much to lose to risk letting her be ostracised — especially now.

The ringing of her mobile phone reverberated around the flat, making it feel emptier than it ever had. She went over to the work surface of her kitchenette and picked it up, looking at the screen. It was a mobile number she didn't recognise. She wouldn't normally answer unknown numbers, but what if it was the police? The detective — the woman one — had said she'd call her if they needed anything else. Maybe this was her. She should answer it. The last thing she needed was them turning up and chucking her in the back of a police car. That would *not* look good with the neighbours.

Tentatively, she answered the call. 'Hello?'

'How do you feel, Megan?'

The voice was deep, definitely male. But she didn't recognise it.

'Sorry, who's this?' she asked.

'Can you feel the net closing in?'

By now, her heart was racing. She knew exactly what he meant. One or two of the others had made remarks about members of the group being picked off one by one, but this was the first time she'd ever taken it seriously. And in that moment, it dawned on her.

'Charlie, grow the fuck up.'

'Call him.'

'What?'

'Call Charlie.'

'I... I don't want to.'

'You don't want to find out for certain I'm not him?'

She swallowed hard, trying to rack her brains and work out who the caller might be. As she did so, the man continued to talk.

'No, of course you don't. You never were interested in the truth, were you? Only whatever truth suited your narrative. Do you remember how many times you told boys at school your nan had died the night before? The only person I ever knew who had thirty grandmothers. Impressive.'

'Do I know you from school?' she asked, narrowing down her field of suspects.

'Oh I very much doubt it. In fact, I'd say almost certainly not.'

'What do you want?'

'I'm getting it, Megan.'

'What, by trying to scare me?'

'I don't have to try. Walk over to the window.'

Megan's heart lurched. 'What? Why?'

'Walk over to the window.'

'No.'

'Walk over to the window, Megan.'

There was something in his voice which told her she had no option. Slowly, tentatively, she stepped her way in silence towards the window.

'I do like to see fear in your eyes, Megan.'

'You can't see my eyes,' she whispered.

'Oh, I can. They look bluer than ever, set off against that orange top.'

Megan reached for the curtains with both hands and pulled them shut, before taking a few steps back. She knew she should hang up the phone, but she had a worrying feeling that would only make things worse.

'Oh come on, Megan. It's not even dark yet,' the voice said.

'You're scaring me,' she said, her voice cracking.

'Of course I am. How does it feel?'

'How do you think it feels?' she replied, almost yelling.

'I know perfectly well. That's why I want to know how it feels for you. It's your turn, now.'

'Did... Did I do something to you?' she asked, realising this must be the only possible reason someone would be treating her like this. Who had she wronged, upset?

'You really don't know, do you? No, I didn't think you would. In fact, I knew you wouldn't. I know a lot about you, Megan.'

'No you don't.'

'Oh, I do. I know you're holding the phone to your right ear, for example.'

'You just saw me before I closed the curtains,' Megan said, switching the phone into her other hand.

'Now your left ear.'

She span round, looking for another window she knew damn well didn't exist. How could he still see her? He was bluffing. He had to be. He knew which ear she'd been holding the phone up to, and knew there was a good chance she'd switch it after he mentioned the right ear. That's all this was. A bluff. She walked over to the fruit bowl on the work surface of her kitchenette and picked up an orange. 'Okay,' she said. 'What am I holding?'

'It matches your top beautifully, Megan.'

Megan threw the orange back in the bowl and picked up a banana.

'Must be a familiar sensation, that one. Although you're probably used to them feeling somewhat warmer.'

'How are you doing this?' she asked, her voice a whisper. 'Where are you?'

'Watching. As I always have been.'

In that moment, Megan felt less safe than she ever had in

her life. He was here. He could see her. She had to get out, go somewhere, anywhere.

She hung up the phone, reached for her keys and dashed out of the door, not caring for a second that she didn't even have any shoes on. She needed to get out of here as quickly as possible. She didn't know where she'd go, but she knew she had to. She only lived a stone's throw from the town centre. She could sprint to the police station. Anywhere. She just had to be away from here.

She slammed the door to her flat behind her and took the stairs two at a time until she was down on the ground floor. Her heart hammered in her chest as she opened the heavy front door to the building.

Just as she stepped onto the tarmac, a hand clamped itself over her mouth and she was dragged backwards, her heels scraping against the floor as she realised she'd already taken her last breath.

39

If Caroline had been given a pound for every time someone told her a dead body had been discovered by a dog walker, she wouldn't have needed to spend her Saturday mornings looking at dead bodies that'd been discovered by dog walkers.

She smiled inwardly to herself as she realised death had yet again introduced her to what would otherwise be a wonderful place to spend an afternoon walking with her family. She'd been reliably informed that the area of woodland between Oakham and Braunston was affectionately known as Betty's Bottom — another local fact she'd have little trouble forgetting at any point in the future.

When it came to the body, though, Caroline didn't need to wait for formal identification this time. She recognised the corpse immediately.

'It's Megan Wilkes,' she said, as Dexter walked towards her, having only just arrived at the scene.

'Shit.'

'Look.' Caroline pointed towards Megan's neck, where

she'd noticed the scratch marks. To her, they looked defensive, as if she'd been scrabbling to free herself from the noose from which she was hanging.

'Possible last-minute change of mind?' Dexter asked.

Caroline shook her head. 'I don't think so. Anyway, look at the rope.' The loose section of rope which dangled the other side of the multitude of knots was a brown-green colour. 'Scuff marks from the tree,' she said. 'Someone's put the noose round her neck then hauled her up by pulling the rope. That's what's rubbed off the branch and onto the rope.'

Dexter looked up at the tree, but there'd be no way of inspecting the friction damage to the tree until the body had been taken down. He had to admit he didn't know one type of tree from another, but the branch Megan was dangling from was broader than the trunks of most trees.

'She's only a small thing,' he said. 'Wouldn't take Geoff Capes to get her up there.'

As she gradually realised the implications of this, Caroline felt her world beginning to fall apart around her. There could be no doubt as to what they were looking at. This was the same person who'd killed Tom Medland and, she now felt sure, Guy Sherman. That meant they'd suddenly rocketed from one almost-certain murder to three. And that had far more serious, far starker implications: she now officially had a serial killer on her hands.

40

The warmth of the day wasn't helped by the plastic full body coverings Caroline and Dexter had to wear before entering Megan Wilkes's flat. Having been at the scene where her body was found, and still being unsure as to where she was actually killed, they had to tread carefully — both literally and figuratively.

The process of any police investigation needed to ensure that procedure was stuck to rigorously, and that defence counsel wouldn't be given any potential loopholes or avenues to exploit.

It wasn't unheard of for cases to fall apart because it was discovered the same police officer had arrested the defendant and subsequently been involved in searching the crime scene. That was the sort of chink in the armour a defence brief could drive a bus through, pointing out the distinct possibility that the hair or fibre from the suspect found at the scene might not have been left during a murder, but inadvertently and accidentally transferred by the police officer.

It was a stretch to claim this, of course, but entirely possible. And in circumstances where a court jury is told they must only delivery a guilty verdict when they can be absolutely certain of the defendant's guilt *beyond all reasonable doubt*, this was exactly the sort of situation in which a case could collapse immediately.

As they assembled in the car park of the block of flats where Megan Wilkes lived, Caroline looked around her.

'Is there any sign of forced entry to her flat?' she asked the buildings manager, who'd introduced himself as Nigel Gibbs.

'No, nothing,' Gibbs said. 'Her front door wasn't locked, but some people don't. You can't get into the flats from the outside without a key anyway.'

'And what about the building itself? Would someone need to be buzzed in?'

'Unless they pressed the "Trades" button, yeah. That'd let them straight into the lobby. We can get CCTV footage from the car park, but there's nothing on the building itself because most of the flats are privately owned to one extent or another.'

Caroline nodded and thanked him. 'You ready?' she asked Dexter, as they prepared to enter the building.

'As I'll ever be.'

The unspoken but clear atmosphere now seemed to be that it was inevitable EMSOU would get involved. There'd be little chance of anything else, especially with a rising death toll and no clear suspect whatsoever.

Megan's flat was neat and tidy, and tastefully furnished even if it was clear she hadn't spent a great deal of money on it.

Almost as soon as they entered, a forensics officer

approached them clutching an evidence bag containing a mobile phone. Caroline recognised it as one of the more recent iPhones, but she couldn't have said which model.

'Is it locked?' she asked.

'Four-digit PIN code,' the officer replied.

Caroline took the bag and pressed the side button of the phone through the plastic. The screen came to life, a picture of Megan and Tom on a beach somewhere, the current time superimposed on the tops of their heads, with a couple of Instagram notifications in the middle of the screen. She swiped up the screen to unlock the phone, seeing the PIN entry screen.

'What year was she born?' Caroline asked Dexter.

'Dunno. She was, what, thirty-two?'

Caroline tapped the numbers 1-9-8-8 into the phone through the plastic evidence bag. The screen unlocked. 'Every time,' she said. 'Every bloody time.' She navigated to the Messages app and flicked through, but there was nothing out of the ordinary. It seemed she rarely sent or received text messages – a sign of another keen WhatsApper. Caroline opened WhatsApp on the phone and immediately saw that her most recent conversation from the previous evening was with Charlie Ford.

He'd sent her the first message:

Bored and lonely... you free? x

Megan's response couldn't have been clearer:

After last time? No chance.

So who killed her? There was no sign of forced entry in the flat, so did she know her killer and let him in? Or had she gone out of her own accord and been killed while she was out?

In that case, where had she gone? Who had she gone to meet? And why did she leave her phone at home? Either way, one thing was almost certain: Megan Wilkes wasn't their murderer. She was now the latest victim.

Had Charlie reacted badly to her message and killed her? That made no sense to Caroline. It wasn't strong enough. In any case, they'd be able to check the CCTV from the car park and — she hoped — see if anyone had made their way into the building that way.

For Caroline, attention now turned back to Alex Lawson. Was he their man after all? Had he panicked that Megan might blow his cover and land him in it? But try as she might, she couldn't quite see Alex being released from custody, then almost immediately killing Megan. It was almost too convenient, but they'd do their due diligence in making sure that was the case.

These were the questions she was forcing herself to focus on, because there was one enormous dark question at the back of her mind which scared her far more: How on earth was she going to deal with Rutland's first serial killer?

41

Caroline assembled her team in the incident room and relayed the latest information to them. Part of her felt bad at having dragged them all in at the weekend, but it was fair to say she now had no option. She needed to throw absolutely everything at this, because they either had to identify and apprehend the killer almost immediately, or the higher-ups would take the case from her.

'Guv, we've had something back. It's not good news,' Aidan Chilcott said, looking rather awkward.

Caroline wondered if and when good news would ever come. 'Alright. Go on, Aidan.'

'The initial post-mortem's back on Guy Sherman. In short, it's inconclusive. They've confirmed he died by hanging and wasn't dead prior to that. They mentioned the fibres under his fingernails, which they said could have been either a change of mind or a potential struggle. Again, inconclusive, but it does mention that there are no other signs of a fight or physical struggle. There's an area of recent pressure on his back, but that could be anything.'

Caroline closed her eyes and nodded. She'd feared as much. Although there'd been nothing on the surface to confirm that Guy Sherman's death had been anything other than suicide, she knew deep down it was too much of a coincidence — especially following the murder of Megan Wilkes.

'So we're seeing plenty of links,' she said, addressing her team. 'The three victims were all from the same group of friends, loosely speaking. We know there were frayed and fractured relationships within that friendship group, but if nothing else, they all knew each other well. So I think we can safely say our killer is someone who knows them all. If we're looking at the tighter group itself, that narrows the field substantially. Alex Lawson, Sophie Lawson and Charlie Ford are the only ones left. I think we probably have to discount Sophie, based on the nature of the crimes. She's a slight little thing. I can't see her hauling Megan Wilkes's body up into a tree, or dragging Tom Medland down that embankment, much less getting into a building site and chucking Guy Sherman off the edge. Both Alex and Charlie have been suspects of ours for various reasons. Ford is a previous customer, but there's nothing to suggest he killed either Tom, Guy or Megan. Nothing, other than a criminal record. Alex Lawson, on the other hand, had plenty of reason to kill Tom as he'd been sleeping with Megan for years. We're not aware of a reason why he'd want to kill Guy, and his motive for killing Megan is pretty weak, other than to keep her quiet following their arrest. Maybe there's something deeper which he was afraid of having revealed.'

'Deeper than murder?' Sara asked.

'Absolutely, Sara. If no-one thought there was anything deeper or darker than murder, no-one would ever get killed, would they? For too many people, there are secrets that are far more important. Money. Love. Revenge. They all go much further than murder for some people. Now, I'm sure there's a link with the car somewhere along the line. The Vauxhall Corsa owned and driven by Megan Wilkes. A Corsa bearing her registration number was seen heading towards the site where Tom Medland's body was discovered. Forensically, we can't prove it was her car until we get results back on the blood. We can't get a match on mud from her tyres, although the tyre marks at Manton are from a Corsa. But at the same time, we know her car didn't leave the car park outside her flat on the night Tom was murdered. I think there might be an explanation for that. It was a Corsa bearing her registration plates, but not her Corsa.'

'You mean someone stole them?' Dexter asked.

Caroline shook her head. 'Too risky. Possible, but too risky. My theory is that someone had a new set of registration plates made up. Safest option would be a friendly local workshop who'd be willing to do it off the record, but that's a lot harder nowadays than it was. But go online and there are dozens of companies willing to make what they call show plates. Basically, you can get anything made up on a number plate. Your own name, a word, whatever. There's a legal disclaimer on the site which says you can't use the plate on the road, but there's nothing to stop anyone from doing that. My theory is that our killer used one of those sites to get replicas of Megan's Corsa plates made up, which he then put on an identical vehicle, which was used for the murder of Tom Medland. Aidan, can you check out those online sellers and retailers of show plates, please? Get them to check their records and see if they've sold plates bearing Megan Wilkes's registration number at any point.'

As she spoke, Caroline heard her office phone ringing. As much as she didn't want to, she knew she should answer it. She was half-expecting a call inviting her into a meeting in which she'd be told Operation Utopia was being handed up the food chain, but it could just as well be a vital piece of evidence coming in, or a witness with some information which could land Caroline her killer. 'Sorry, one moment,' she said. 'Dex, can you fill in for a minute or two please?'

She stepped into her office and closed the door behind her, before picking up the phone. 'DI Hills.'

'Ah, hi,' said a friendly female voice at the other end of the phone. 'My name's Leah MacGregor, I'm a reporter with the Rutland and Stamford Mercury. Have you got a couple of minutes for me please?'

Caroline sighed. It was an inevitable part of the job that the press would be keen to get their information on crimes happening locally. It made for good news stories, of course, but it wasn't just sheer sensationalism. The relationship between the police and press was key, as more often than not the coverage a crime got would lead to witnesses coming forward with information which helped progress cases. It was something which needed to be carefully handled, though, and at that moment in time Caroline wasn't sure she had the time or the patience. 'I really don't, sorry. Can you call back tomorrow please?'

'Is that wise?' Leah MacGregor asked.

'Sorry?'

'Well, there could be another victim by then, couldn't there?'

Caroline felt her heart racing as she listened to the reporter's question. 'Sorry,' she said, trying to play the innocent. 'I'm not quite sure what you mean.'

'Oh? That's strange,' Leah MacGregor said. 'Because the story we're hearing is that Rutland has its first serial killer.'

42

Sophie Lawson's hands shook with terror as she watched Alex leave again. This time, though, he hadn't been angry at her.

He'd come back late last night and hadn't said a word about pinning her up against the wall. She wasn't about to bring it up, either. She'd already seen what he was capable of when he was under pressure.

That was Alex's problem, she'd come to realise. He'd never been under pressure before. Not really. He claimed his job was stressful, but it wasn't. It was just busy. For the first time in his life, the walls were closing in on him and he didn't know how to handle it. That wasn't his fault. But when she'd seen him resort to violence as his only answer, she knew he wasn't the person she'd married.

He didn't seem like a man who was panicking because he was about to be caught as a serial killer; he seemed more like a man who was panicking because he thought he might be the next victim. But then again, she couldn't say that for sure. How many serial killers did she know? She'd already seen what a bad judge of character she'd been, looking solely at Alex's behaviour yesterday.

She'd felt a growing distance from her husband for some time, but had never quite been able to put her finger on it. She'd felt like a hanger-on, an incidental part of Alex's life, and that she was merely coming along for the ride. He'd always been so focused on his work and moving on in his career, and at the start she'd admired that. She'd thought maybe he was doing it for her and their future family. But as time had gone on, she'd come to realise his desire for money was just about all there was to him. Everything else fed into his ego and his need to keep moving on.

Was that what this was all about? Had his arrest and interview bruised his ego in such a way that he didn't know how to handle it? That still didn't tell her whether her husband was a serial killer. Wasn't narcissism meant to be a classic sign?

Right now, she desperately wanted to get out. Not just out of the house; out of the marriage, out of everything. But where could she go? She had no money, nothing of her own to speak of. The logical step would be to go to her mum's, but she was genuinely frightened of Alex finding her there. That realisation was what told her she needed to get away from this man, for once and for all. And, knowing where he'd gone and what he was likely to do, she had an idea as to how she might manage it.

She picked up her mobile phone, then looked at the small piece of card before carefully, with shaking hands, dialling the number that was printed on it.

43

Alex Lawson was thinking of nothing other than kicking Charlie Ford's head in. If the police weren't going to take him seriously and arrest the scumbag, what other choice did he have? In any case, choices weren't looking like a luxury when it came to dealing with Charlie Ford.

Alex pulled his car up on the country lane and looked again at the message on his phone. Charlie's taunts and threats had been clear: He wanted Alex to know that he wasn't the only one who'd been having his fun with Megan, and that he was perfectly willing to let Sophie know that too. It was a message that had enraged Alex and, he felt sure, was designed to stop him from urging the police to investigate Charlie. But if Charlie thought that's how Alex was going to react to threats like that, he could think again.

He drove a little further up the lane before pulling into the farmland just outside Tinwell, where Charlie Ford lived in his glorified cattle shed. Not that there was much glory about it, even when compared to a shitty one. Feeling the rage swelling inside him, he opened his car door, stepped out onto the gravel and locked up the car. If Charlie wanted to play the big man, he could damn well do it face to face, like a proper man.

He wasn't afraid of his record. He knew the real truth — that Charlie's assault convictions were times when he'd decided to pick a fight with the smallest, weakest, drunkest guys in the pub. It was hardly a sign that he was any sort of big man, despite what he liked to claim.

Alex marched up to the front of Charlie's shithole and hammered his fist on the door. He wanted the man to be under no illusion that he meant business. A few moments later, the door opened and Charlie appeared in the entrance, clad in a white vest and shorts, looking as though he hadn't washed in weeks. Alex shoved both hands into the man's chest, pushing him backwards, before launching himself at him and raining punches on him, just as he heard the tyres on gravel and the gentle *whoop-whoop* of the police officers tapping their sirens to announce their arrival.

44

With Alex Lawson being carted away in handcuffs by PC Joe Lloyd, Caroline closed the front door to Charlie's farmhouse and sat down on the sofa opposite him.

'Are you sure you don't want to get that looked at? I really think you should go to the hospital.'

'I'll be fine. He barely touched me,' Charlie said.

Usually, Caroline would try to talk an assault victim into getting their injuries looked at, but she could see Charlie Ford wasn't going to change his mind.

'So, what was that all about?' she said to Charlie, nodding and smiling at Dexter as he walked into the room.

'No idea. Your guess is as good as mine.'

'What, so you've got no idea why a friend of yours turned up at your home out of the blue and attacked you? Did he say anything?'

'Nothing. Just went for me the second I opened the door.'

'Okay. Now, I'm not one to interfere in people's private lives, but let me tell you what we do know. We know that

Megan Wilkes and Alex Lawson had been seeing each other for a couple of years, on and off. We also know you attempted to "see" Megan yesterday evening. In fact, that's the last contact she's known to have had with anyone at this stage. Do you think I might be on the right page when it comes to reasons why Alex might've wanted to harm you?'

'Woah. Hang on a sec. I never texted Megan. Who told you I did?'

'No-one needs to tell us anything, Charlie. We have her phone. We've seen the messages.'

'Don't think so somehow. I'm telling you now I haven't texted Megan in ages. Look at my phone if you want.'

Caroline declined. She knew how easy it was for people to delete messages from their own phones and try to claim they hadn't sent them in the first place. 'We can ask your network provider to give us a log of all messages, you know.'

Charlie shrugged. 'Do what you like. I know I didn't send her anything.'

Caroline made a note to have someone check the records. That'd prove once and for all whether Charlie was telling the truth, which could easily open up a can of worms. 'So are you saying that you and Megan haven't been seeing each other at all?' she asked.

Charlie shuffled awkwardly. 'Well no, I'm not saying that. I'm just saying I didn't send her no messages.'

'And how do you think Alex would react to finding that out? He and Megan had been close, hadn't they?'

Charlie shrugged. 'Dunno about that. They'd been shagging, yeah, but who hasn't shagged Megan? She's hardly the sort of girl anyone's going to get possessive over. And anyway,

Alex was married to Sophie, so he's not exactly gonna start getting angry over someone else seeing his bit on the side, is he?'

'I don't know,' Caroline said. 'That's why I'm asking you.'

'Nah. He's not like that.'

'What is he like, then?'

Charlie sighed. 'Listen, I haven't got time for all this, alright? I just want to leave it there. I don't want to press charges.'

Caroline tried not to laugh, but a small chuckle escaped her lips. 'I'm afraid it doesn't quite work like that. Despite what you might see on the telly, we don't "press charges" in this country. It's entirely down to the police to choose whether to investigate a crime, and completely down to the CPS if they want to authorise a charge. Individuals don't get a say in the matter.'

Charlie shrugged again. 'Alright. Do what you like. I'm past caring, to be honest.'

Caroline looked at Charlie Ford, and she could tell those words were the biggest truth he'd spoken in a long time.

45

'We're missing something, Dex,' Caroline said, pacing her office. 'I don't know what, but there's got to be something we don't know that holds this whole thing together. Why would someone want to kill their friends? Even with their bizarre group dynamic, it just doesn't fit for me.'

'No weirder than a third party wanting to pick off the whole group. How can you have a vendetta against that many people?' Dexter replied.

Caroline sat down in her chair. 'I know,' she said. 'That's what makes me think we're missing a vital piece here.'

'Got to agree. And I think there's a trend. I reckon it's got to be linked to the suicide pact thing we looked at.'

'Oh come on, Dex. We know for a fact they were killed. What are you saying? They're all killing each other in turn, like some sort of elongated version of *Strangers on a Train*?'

'Well, no, although that's not a bad idea. Think about it. Guy kills Tom. He was strong enough. Megan then kills Guy by shoving him off the building. She'd have been strong enough for that one. Then someone else killed Megan.'

'Who?'

'Whoever's next to die.'

'Oh, great. We'll just sit and wait it out, then. And why would they go to all that trouble, knowing they were only going to get murdered a couple of days later?'

'It's not my theory, guv. You're the one who said it.'

'No, I... Look, forget it. I shouldn't have said anything. What's your theory?'

'Well, what if our killer is using methods that look like suicide for a reason? What if *that* is the message? He's using the same method each time, even though he knows by now that *we* know it's not suicide. It's got to mean something.'

'But why? And why them?'

'I don't know,' Dexter said, sighing. 'But there's got to be a link. It's not just that they're old school friends and kept in touch over the years. It can't be. It doesn't make sense. Not quite, anyway. Like you say, we're missing something. The real link.'

Caroline slowly nodded. 'Alright, Dex. Alright. I think I've got an idea.'

46

Caroline knocked on the door of Chief Superintendent Derek Arnold's office and waited for him to call her in.

Once she was inside, she sat down on the chair in front of his desk and explained the situation to him. She'd been amazed he hadn't called her in before now, and didn't know whether that was a good thing or not. Too often in policing, things went on behind closed doors and plans were put into action, and the last people to find out were those who were most closely affected.

'Either way,' she said, coming to the end of her explanation, 'we're pretty certain one of two things will happen. Either one of the remaining three members of the group is the killer, or their lives are in grave danger.'

Arnold seemed to take this in the spirit in which Caroline had intended it, and nodded slowly. 'I see,' he said, steepling his hands in front of his chin. 'I see.'

'In my opinion, I think we need to set up covert surveillance on Alex Lawson, Sophie Lawson and Charlie

Ford. If the patterns are right, over the next day or two, one of them will either kill or be killed.'

'Covert surveillance?' Arnold asked, raising an eyebrow.

'Yeah. We'll need resources, of course, but I honestly think it's the only way we can stop more deaths and find our killer.'

Derek Arnold made a noise which sounded like someone piercing a whoopee cushion with a toothpick. 'You realise those resources would have to be external? Or regional, at least.'

'You mean EMSOU.'

'I mean EMSOU. They're not going to take kindly to being asked to provide valuable resources to prop up your investigation, just because you decided you wanted to keep it local. Just to pre-empt what they're going to say. Not my words, of course,' he said, raising his hands in mock surrender on seeing the look on Caroline's face.

'And they should be professional enough to supply resources where they're needed in order to stop a potential murder taking place. And yes, those are my words.'

'Oh, I quite agree. But I'm sure you can understand that I'm forced to act as a sort of mediator here. It's proving diffi-cult, to say the least, to keep having to persuade them that this is the best way to do things. I don't think you have any idea how much work it takes to keep making exceptions for you.'

Caroline swallowed, feeling the pressure starting to rise inside her again. She felt stuck. She tended to put more than enough pressure on herself to get results and do things the right way, so being stymied by the higher-ups and forces outside of her control took an unnecessary toll. She couldn't tell Arnold that, though. If he got any sniff that she was unable to cope or that the case was having a knock-on effect on her physical health, the case would be pulled from her in no time. Frankly, she was amazed it hadn't been already.

'So is that a no?' Caroline asked.

Arnold raised his hands. 'I'm quite happy to say yes, Caroline. You know I am. I'm just letting you know the predicament I'm in. By rights, and by generally accepted procedure, EMSOU should be handling the case.'

'With respect, sir, I've read the guidance and the documentation. They're there to provide support and consolidated resources for major crimes. There's nothing that says we're obliged to let them take over every major crime investigation.'

'I know what they'll say. I know what the conditions will be. It's all politics. The decision has to be yours, Caroline. Do you want me to call them in?'

A COUPLE OF MINUTES LATER, Caroline hurried across the car park to her Volvo, feeling the weight of every step as her weakened body fought to keep her upright.

Her consultant had told her she needed to keep external stresses to a minimum because her body wouldn't react well in her current situation. What he hadn't told her is how quickly she'd see the damage it caused.

She sat in the driver's seat, one leg still hanging out, unable to summon the strength to close the door for another minute or two, feeling the breeze whipping across the front of her face. She took some deep breaths, calmed her heart rate, then closed the door — opening the window for fresh air — and started the car.

She needed to be at home. She hated leaving her team in the lurch, but she wouldn't be far away. She was there if they needed her, even though she knew they wouldn't.

As she reached Ashwell Road and passed the convenience store, a sudden wave of nausea hit her. She pulled the car over as quickly as she could, its rear end sticking out into the road, opened the door and managed to lean just far enough out to avoid ruining the interior of her car.

Thankful there was no other traffic, but aware of the look of disdain on the face of the elderly gentleman who'd been pruning his privet hedge on the other side of the road, Caroline closed the car door and continued on home.

47

Caroline woke the next morning having slept like a log for twelve hours straight. Heavy stress tended to make her a light sleeper, and she took it as a sign of her weakening body that she'd gone to bed so early and managed to get so much solid sleep at a time of such high stress.

She'd been awake barely ten or fifteen minutes when Dexter called, his name flashing up on her mobile while she was reading a news article about medical trials for lymphoma treatment. She was busily wondering if there might be aspects that could be used in treating other cancers — ovarian at the forefront of her mind — when she answered his call.

'Morning, guv. Didn't manage to catch you before you went home last night, but I wanted to let you know we've had a visit.'

'Dex, are you in the office?' she asked, glancing at the clock on her bedside table.

'Yeah. Why?'

'Just wondered if there was any point in you going home

every night, that's all. Might as well pop a tent up in the car park.'

Dexter laughed. 'Not gonna lie, the thought had crossed my mind. Now. The visit.'

'Let me guess,' Caroline said. 'EMSOU?'

'Yeah. Sorry.'

'It's alright. I knew.'

'Oh? Oh. That's why you went home early.'

'Don't worry. It's okay. They're helping us out and providing resources, but I'm still the SIO.'

Dexter made a murmuring noise. 'I wonder how long that'll last.'

'I'm assured it'll remain the case, Dex. Don't worry.' It was important to her that her team didn't concern themselves over a loss of autonomy and that she showed them confidence, even though privately she had very much the same worries they did.

'Are you in today?'

'Yeah. Yeah I will be. I'll be there in an hour or so. Can you pile up the sandbags and nail the doors shut until then?'

'Uh. You serious?'

'No, Dex. Welcome them. Make them a coffee. But make sure you use the crap stuff Aidan got from that corner shop.'

KNOWING she had to keep her stress levels to a minimum, Caroline forced herself to put on a brave face. There was nothing she could do. She had to accept the regional operation would likely put pressure on her to do things their way.

They'd want to take credit when the killer was identified too, she was sure. She could see how it was going to play out from a mile off. Even if she caught the killer single-handed — again — it'd be at least heavily hinted that the real breakthrough only came when EMSOU's resources were deployed.

For her, the main thing was that the killer was found. It had to be one of the remaining group members: Alex Lawson, Sophie Lawson or Charlie Ford. Another of them would be the next to die. By making sure all three were under permanent surveillance, the next victim would be protected and the killer would be identified.

But what if the killer was either Alex or Sophie, and their spouse was next on the list? Caroline couldn't see any way in which a surveillance team — even if they were sitting right outside the house or hiding out underneath the kitchen sink — would be able to stop the assailant before their next victim was dead. And all the while she was still the Senior Investigating Officer in charge of the case.

She gritted her teeth as she figured the higher-ups had probably come to this realisation long before she had. They must have known the risks and the various permutations and taken a calculated gamble: if it worked, they could take the credit; if it failed, Caroline was the officer in charge and the person responsible.

Far from feeling relieved or thankful for the additional support, although she knew it was vital and necessary, she was already starting to feel squeezed and penned in by the pressure and the knowledge of what was to come.

48

He loved a creature of habit. They were so much easier to keep an eye on. Predictable, too. You always knew where they'd be, and when. Even if their schedules tended to vary, like hers did, there were still plenty of elements he could rely on.

Take now, for example. He watched as she got into her Volvo, reversed out onto her street, then turned onto Ashwell Road, driving past his car as she did so. He pulled his Ford Focus out onto the road a little way behind her, keeping enough distance but also ensuring she stayed well within his sight.

Sometimes he'd pull out of a side road. Other days, he'd be waiting further up or down the road. On occasion, he'd even be on foot or riding a motorbike. He had no shortage of vehicles or places to leave them. And who ever looked at the person driving a car? All anyone ever paid any attention to was the car itself. Of course, he changed his appearance as much as he could using a selection of hats, glasses and false beards, but it really wasn't necessary. She hadn't noticed him once yet, and he'd been keeping an eye on her for a while. Quite poor form for a copper, he thought. And a Detective Inspector at that.

He'd been keeping a close eye on Caroline Hills ever since she'd been put in charge of the investigation. He needed to know what she knew, watch where she went, see who she spoke to. He couldn't have her getting too close to the truth. Not yet. He still wasn't finished.

Once he'd killed his final victim, he wouldn't care. In fact, he'd probably hand himself in. There wouldn't be much point in anything after that. His only reason for living was to see them all dead.

For a short while, he thought he'd fallen at the first hurdle. He'd planned as much as he could for as long as he could, and he'd almost mucked it up. In the end, though, it had worked like a dream. He'd hoped Tom would've gone down as a suicide, but that was all history now. It looked as though he'd got away with it when it came to Guy, although he had no idea how. He'd been extremely careful to cover his tracks that time. All things considered, he had to be. Otherwise, they could've got scarily close to the truth.

Megan had been a risk, but it was a risk that needed taking. By then the police had spoken to three of the group, and it wouldn't be long before someone joined the dots and traced them back to him. And that's why he needed to act fast. That's why he had to keep an eye on Detective Inspector Caroline Hills. He'd waited years for this moment, and he wasn't about to let her ruin it for him before he was finished. His next victim had to die soon, before the net closed in. And if Detective Inspector Caroline Hills got in the way, he'd have no choice but to make sure she was next.

49

Caroline pulled into the entry road for the police station and noticed a woman standing in front of the gate, blocking her entry. Seeing the steely look in the woman's eye and knowing she wasn't about to move, Caroline turned the car engine off and stepped out onto the path. As she did so, a Ford Focus crawled along Station Road behind her.

'Excuse me, this area needs to be kept clear. It's an entry and exit point for emergency police vehicles.'

The woman smiled and held out her hand. 'Leah MacGregor. Rutland and Stamford Mercury. I was hoping you might have a couple of minutes to answer some questions.'

'Were you?' Caroline asked, realising this was the reporter who'd called her the other day. She looked at her outstretched hand and left her hanging. 'Well I'm afraid you'll have to make an appointment. You can't just doorstep us on our way to work.'

'Is it true that Operation Utopia is now a serial killer

investigation? Do you believe the person responsible has murdered three separate people?'

'You know I can't go into operational details with you, Leah. Anything that'd be in the public interest will be released through the usual channels in due course. Now, if you don't mind.'

'Surely it's in the public interest to know there's a serial killer in Rutland, is it not? What good reason could there be for keeping that from the general public, DI Hills?'

Caroline swallowed. 'You're working on the assumption that's the case.'

'Are you telling me it isn't?'

'I'm telling you you're going to need to move out of the way, because we need to clear this area and I need to get into work.'

'Can you confirm for the record there definitely *isn't* a serial killer operating in Rutland?'

'You can't prove a negative, Leah. You know that.'

'So there might be?'

'No, I didn't say that. Since when do local journalists work Sundays, anyway? We have enough trouble getting hold of them at five past five on a weekday.'

'This story's going to run, Detective Inspector. It's in the public interest. People aren't going to feel safe. I don't want a backlash or mass hysteria any more than you do. That's why I'm so keen to get the facts rather than just speculating. Don't you think it'd be best to set the record straight properly, so you can control the narrative?'

Caroline was stuck between a rock and a hard place. If she agreed, it'd become public knowledge that Rutland had its first ever serial killer. If she declined, MacGregor could run the story anyway, and fill in with her own opinions and speculation. And although she knew the Mercury — as Britain's oldest newspaper — was one of the most esteemed and trustworthy publications around, tight control over communications was absolutely key when it came to cases like this, and she couldn't afford even the slightest risk of incorrect information getting out.

'Alright. Have you got a card? I'll get a press conference organised as soon as possible. I'll make sure you get the first question.'

'No limits?'

Caroline clenched her jaw and gave a small nod. 'No limits.'

50

They must've thought he was stupid. How could they possibly think he wouldn't notice them? They couldn't have looked more obvious if they tried. If they were there as a visual deterrent, it could be argued they might be successful. But he wasn't going to be deterred.

He'd been ultra-aware of his surroundings for some time now, and felt both humoured and angry at seeing the man and woman sitting in an unmarked BMW down the road from Sophie's mum's house. Did they really think he was thick enough to not notice them? It was almost insulting. The good news, though, was that they didn't seem to have noticed him. That said it all, as far as he was concerned. He was a hundred times better at this surveillance malarkey than they were.

He noticed the front-door of Sophie's mum's house opening. But it wasn't the door he was watching. Nor was it Sophie. He was watching the two people sitting in the car further up the road, noticing how excited and animated they got, all the while completely unaware of his presence.

He hated the Volkswagen e-up! with a passion. Even its name was stupid. But it was perfect for the job. He turned the key to start the car, an audible *ping-pong* letting him know the electric motor was now active. He clicked the car into drive and hovered his foot over the accelerator pedal. He'd need to time this perfectly. He'd had a lot of practice with the car and had a good idea of when he'd need to floor it. From this direction, Sophie would walk across the street to her car, diagonally and away from him. She wouldn't hear the car until it was too late. But he had to get it right.

He turned his attention to her, watching as she walked down her mother's front path and opened the gate. The moment her foot first hit the—

He was off. She was on the pavement, and the VW was moving forward. Just another second and she'd be crossing the road, not noticing him moving slowly, lights off, ready to floor it.

She gave a quick glance to her right — not long enough to take anything in, and purely through habit — then she was on the asphalt. He knew he only had a couple of seconds. He pressed his foot hard against the accelerator pedal, feeling the car's eighty-odd horsepower doing what it could, watching the gap narrow between them.

Then, in the split-second before the collision, Sophie turned her head in his direction and looked straight at him.

That millisecond seemed to last an age, and he could have sworn Sophie looked straight into his soul. All she would've seen was a pair of eyes peering out from under the baseball cap, a false beard covering the rest of his face. There's no way she'd recognise him. Surely not.

She moved — *shit* — but not enough for him to miss her entirely. There was a thud as the car clipped her, knocking her to the ground.

He didn't slow down, didn't stop, didn't look behind him. He knew exactly where he had to get to, and he had to get there fast.

51

Caroline had spent much of Sunday finalising their approach for the next morning's press conference. Although she had done plenty before as part of her role in the Met, it was a new approach for Rutland Police, who'd barely had a murder to deal with in the years before she joined.

Getting the messaging right was crucial. They needed to ensure the general public were suitably concerned to rack their brains for any information that might help, but at the same time they didn't want to cause unnecessary panic and alarm. After all, Caroline was certain the next victim would be either Alex Lawson, Sophie Lawson or Charlie Ford. For the other 40,000 Rutlanders, there was no need for undue distress. It was a fine line, and one which needed treading carefully.

The rest of the day had been spent briefing the EMSOU surveillance team on what they knew so far, and gearing up to start immediate surveillance on Charlie Ford and the Lawsons. They'd be watched not only physically, but digitally.

Their phones would be monitored for any incoming or outgoing calls and text messages, and their live locations would be tracked. That side of things probably wouldn't do much good — it hadn't for any of the previous victims — and Caroline felt sure that traditional visual surveillance would prove key to catching their killer. But as she answered her phone that evening, she was brought down to earth with a crash.

'You're fucking kidding me,' Caroline said as Chief Super-intendent Derek Arnold relayed the news to her.

'I wish I was.'

'How the hell did that happen? I thought they were meant to be watching her?'

'They were. They watched the whole thing,' Arnold replied. 'The car flew past them at a rate of knots, hit Sophie Lawson, then carried on going. They couldn't pursue the car because she was lying in the middle of the road. They put an immediate call out, but there's been no trace of the car.'

'Shit. What about the reg plate?'

'Goes back to some old boy in Peterborough. Car was tucked up nice and snug under his car port twenty minutes later, gleaming and sparkling new. It isn't the car we want.'

'Cloned plates?'

'Looks like it.'

Caroline sighed. Another falsified registration number. The methods and style of the killer were becoming clear, but his identity was still as unknown as it'd ever been. In theory, two sets of cloned plates should help them enormously. If they could track down the manufacturer of them, they'd be able to cross-reference both orders and — hopefully — discover the identity of the killer. But Caroline had a horrible feeling it wouldn't be that simple. So far, the killer had proven to be clever. He was forensically aware, at least, and appeared to have chosen his victims and planned his murders in advance. But how much exactly did he know?

A bolt of terror shot through Caroline. What if there were very good reasons why their killer was forensically aware, planned in advance and seemed to know what the police were going to do at every step? What if he was... No, she couldn't entertain that possibility.

'How is she now?' Caroline asked.

'She'll be okay. She took quite a wallop, but landed the right way. Could've been a whole lot worse. Got away with lots of bruises, from what I've been told.'

A thought passed Caroline's mind, and in that moment she was able to articulate the thought that'd been floating on the edge of her consciousness since the start of this conversation, but which hadn't been fully formed until now.

'That's a point,' she said. 'Why did they call you?'

'I'm not sure what you mean.'

'I'm still the SIO. Why didn't the call come in to me?'

'I don't know. Maybe they couldn't get hold of you.'

'You managed.'

'I don't know, Caroline. You'd have to ask them.'

'Is there any point? We both know the answer, sir. They didn't want to have to come to me with their tail between their legs.'

'I'm not sure that makes any more sense, to be honest. Surely it'd be worse for them to have to come to me. I'm your senior officer.'

'Yes, but you're a friendly face to them. I'm the renegade maverick from London who thinks she can handle things herself.'

'And which part of that would be incorrect?' Arnold asked, his smile audible in the way he spoke.

'It's not the point, sir. They can't just go above my head because they're too afraid or embarrassed to call me and admit they messed up the second they stepped onto the scene.'

Arnold sighed. 'I'll have a word. And Caroline?'

'Sir.'

'Please leave that bit to me, alright?'

52

There were times when Caroline resented having to bare all to her therapist, and then there were times when she was thankful Rachel was there, able to organise and accommodate a session at short notice when Caroline felt she needed it.

Her pessimistic, negative side told her this was because Rachel knew she couldn't force Caroline to talk, so by actively coming to her for help at times of crisis, it showed Caroline's willingness to deal with the issues at hand. But she'd learned enough from working with Rachel to know this was an unreasonable assumption, and that it would be far more positive and rewarding to assume that Rachel simply cared.

'I'm sorry about Friday,' she said, after the usual greetings were done.

'It's fine,' Rachel replied, smiling. 'We don't need to cover anything that makes you uncomfortable. That's not the purpose at all, I can promise you.'

'I know. But me feeling uncomfortable about things isn't

going to help either. There are things I know I need to address. I've spent my life mentally running away from things, and I know I need to talk. But it's not always as easy as that, is it?'

'No, you're right. Especially when things have been kept to one side or buried for so long. It must be difficult to address them. But that can all come in good time.'

Caroline nodded slowly. In many ways, she felt ready. It was necessary. But she was thankful that Rachel wasn't pushing her towards it.

'So how's work been? You mentioned when we spoke last that it'd been difficult for you. You said you'd been under pressure.'

'Much the same, I guess.' Caroline thought about this for a moment. 'No, actually that's not true. I feel like I've failed. I feel like I've not been able to make the mark, and because of that at least one life has been lost and someone else is in hospital.'

'Why do you think that's because of you?' Rachel asked.

'Because I wasn't able to catch the person responsible in time.'

'I think there are potentially some more helpful ways of framing that. I think most people would agree the only person responsible for someone's death is their killer. You didn't injure anyone. You didn't kill anyone.'

Caroline felt her anxiety rising. 'I was responsible, though. I should have been able to stop it. I was the one who had the job of finding out who it was and having them brought to charge. And I failed in that.'

'You haven't failed. You just haven't succeeded yet.'

'And because of that, people are dead and injured.'

'I think the drive to succeed is a good thing. And of course I'm no expert on policing, but I do know it's a team effort. And from what I know of you, I know you don't do things by halves. I don't imagine for one minute you haven't thrown everything at this. Has anyone ever said to you it's your fault?'

'Well, no. But there've been remarks and things.'

'Can you think of any examples?'

'Well, they've expanded the team. We've got the higher-ups in from regional to help.'

'Is that a bad thing? It sounds like they're doing all they can to help you and make sure you find the person responsible.'

'I... I kind of asked them to, as well.'

'It sounds like they're giving you the resources you need. It sounds to me like they're supporting you as best as possible. It doesn't sound like anyone's blaming you for anything.'

Caroline looked at the painting on the wall above Rachel's head. 'Yeah. Well, I'm blaming myself.'

'Why?'

'Because I always do.'

'Why do you think that is?'

'I dunno. Guilt complex.'

'And what do you think drives that? Why do you think you feel the need to feel guilty about things, even if they're not strictly within your control?'

Caroline thought about this for a few moments. Deep down, she knew exactly why. The only difficulty she had was putting it into words. Before she knew it, beads of sweat had started to appear on her forehead and her hands had begun to tremble.

'It's okay,' Rachel said, her soothing voice providing a calming respite as Caroline's memories took over and she found herself beginning to talk.

53

The first sound was the wailing of her mother. The plane hummed gently in the distance, its low murmur drowned out by her mother's sobs and the trickle of the water over the edges of the rocks.

Her father stood silent, his eyes locked onto the ground where his son had lain, the flickering blue of the ambulance lights playing off his now-pale features.

The paramedic closed the rear doors gently, delicately. In that moment, she wondered why. What was the point? It wouldn't disturb him. It was too late. It had always been too late.

The sunlight danced across the water as it continued to roil and flow, as if oblivious to what had happened. The birds kept singing. The crickets kept chirruping. The trees kept swaying. It was as if nothing had happened, as though the world carried on without them. Without him.

Their world had stopped. They wouldn't know it yet for sure, but it was tangible. She could taste it. There would only be Before and After. She swung between desperation to reverse what had happened — a fraught and anguished need to hit the reset button — and an almost calm, melancholic acceptance that this was now how things were. He wasn't coming back. He was gone.

Dead.

'We'll need to ask you a few questions, if that's okay,' the police officer said.

Her blood ran cold. This was it. It was the first realisation that things could get worse. Much worse. She turned her head and went to speak, but the officer spoke again.

'Mr Spencer?'

Her father jolted at the sound of his name. 'Oh. Yes. Yes, of course. I don't know... I mean, where...'

'We can go somewhere else if you'd feel more comfortable.'

'I wouldn't feel comfortable anywhere. I mean... We just...'

'We'll need to speak to your daughter, too,' the officer said, as if she wasn't even there.

'Yes. Yes, of course. Would... I mean, do you need us to...'

'You should probably be there. Considering her age, and all.'

'She's twelve.'

'I know. You should probably be there.'

'I can be there. I can... I mean, I don't know where. I just...'

'It's okay. Take your time. We just need to establish a chain of events.'

A chain of events. That's all it was. Not the end of a life. Not the death of a child. Not her brother drowning when she should have been taking care of him. It was just a chain of events. One event, then another event, then one more event. A chain.

'Yes,' her father said. 'Yes, I understand. We can... We might as well... I mean...'

'Caroline?' the officer said, looking at her. 'Are you able to tell us what happened?'

Before she knew it, she was nodding.

'Was it just you and Stuart here?' the officer asked.

She wondered whether she should tell them about The Boy From Plot 22. Harry. What good would it do? What would it change? She looked at the officer's uniform, taking in the letters on the badge, and realised in that moment the truth was the only option. Slowly, she shook her head.

'No,' her father said. 'I was here too. I was with them. Stuie got caught in the current. He... There was nothing anyone could have done.'

'You were here?' the officer asked him.

He nodded his head. 'I was.'

The officer looked at her, eyebrows narrowed slightly, as if trying to deduce the truth by looks alone. 'I thought you said your parents weren't here at the time?' the officer asked her.

'We've just established Mr Spencer was here and there was nothing anyone could have done,' the more senior officer said from behind, looking her in the eye. 'A freak accident. That's right, isn't it Caroline?'

Caroline nodded, unable to speak.

'There we go, then. There's no need to interrogate Mr Spencer's daughter, Constable. She's been through quite enough.'

The officer nodded his assent. 'Inspector.'

The senior officer walked slowly over to her father, placing a hand on his shoulder. 'I'm so dreadfully sorry for your loss, David. If there's anything we can do.'

'Yes... Yes, I... Thank you,' her father said, taking the man's hand.

54

Caroline headed into work feeling like she had the hangover from hell, even though she'd felt fine before her session with Rachel. To say it hadn't gone entirely the way she'd planned it would be an understatement, but she'd long had the feeling it was coming.

The thing that had struck her most was Rachel's reaction, or lack of one. All that came was sympathy and empathy, and she felt instantly at ease, free from judgement. Judgement had been her curse ever since Stuie died, even though all judgement had been her own.

She'd seen the power the police had to make everything okay, to help life move on in the only way possible. Of course, things had been far from okay. There'd been days, many days, when she'd been desperate to scream the truth from the rooftops. But what good would it have done? She wasn't entirely sure it had even done any good now she'd told Rachel. The main feeling was a sort of deep fog, a numbness at having bared all. She hoped this was what would gradually become a lighter, freer feeling.

She tried to push through — she had to. She desperately needed to rest, but that could come later. There were three people dead and one in hospital, lucky to be alive. Caroline felt an intense responsibility to provide answers for the family. She knew how gut-wrenching it was to have those truths suppressed.

'So, what do we know?' she asked Dexter, allowing him to take centre stage for a few moments.

'Not a huge amount so far. We know Sophie went to visit her mum at her house in Bourne last night. Her phone was on location monitoring as part of the ongoing surveillance, and a unit was sent up there to watch the house and make sure she stayed in sight. They were parked up a little further down the road, keeping an eye on things. Their account is that they saw her leaving the house, kissing her mum goodbye, then walking down the front path of the property. She walked a little further along the pavement before stepping out into the road. At that point, they became aware of a car speeding towards Sophie with its headlights off. It was still accelerating at the point it clipped Sophie, and afterwards.'

'So it was deliberate?' Caroline asked.

'It seems so, yeah. The car then turns left at the end of the road and back towards the main road. It's caught on CCTV shortly after, passing an industrial unit on the South Fen Road, heading east.'

'What's out there?'

'The Fens.'

'You're joking.'

'I wish I was.'

'So he could be anywhere?' Caroline asked, knowing the chances of finding one car in almost 1,500 square miles of marshland would be impossible. There were roads that followed a straight line through the plains for five miles or more, with hundreds and thousands of tiny dirt tracks jutting off in all directions. The car could be holed up in any one of Christ knows how many barns, farm buildings or smallholdings in an area that covered three counties.

'Pretty much, yeah,' Dexter replied. 'Once you're out there, that's it. There's nothing. No CCTV, no ANPR. But one hell of a lot of hiding places.'

'He's planned this. He waited for her to visit Bourne. He knew exactly where Sophie's mum lived, and he knew he'd be out and heading for the Fens within minutes.'

'Looks that way to me, too. Surveillance team did pick up a reg number, but I think you've been briefed on where that traced back to already. It's probably fair to say that Charles Hartfield-Smythe, ninety-three, of Orton Longueville is not our serial killer.'

'I'll be honest, Dex; nothing would surprise me anymore. But yes, let's scrub him off the list. What else have we got?'

'Alright. On Megan, we've been tracing her recent calls and messages. She received a call on Friday night from a number unfamiliar to her. It hadn't called or texted her before then.'

'Do we know what was said?'

Dexter shook his head. 'No way of knowing, I'm afraid. There's no record of the same number calling any of the others, but if they do we'll be able to hear what's said now they're on monitoring.'

'Any trace on the owner?'

'Three guesses.'

Caroline sighed. 'I'm too tired for guesses, Dex. Let's have the information.'

'Unregistered pay-as-you-go.'

Caroline felt her heart sink. There'd been talk of banning unregistered pay-as-you-go SIMs for some years, but it had never quite come to fruition. As a result, it was still perfectly possible to get hold of a fresh phone and SIM card, a clean mobile phone number with no way of ever being identified as the actual owner.

'We've been trying to do what we can. The network told us the phone was topped up at a village shop just outside Stamford. Cash transaction, no CCTV.'

'Oh for Christ's sake.'

'I know. He's thought about this. He's not leaving anything to chance.'

Whichever way they turned, whatever leads they followed, it seemed to Caroline that their killer was at least one step ahead, if not more. He knew what he was doing. He understood what was traceable and what could lead them to him. And, at every turn, he seemed to know what their next move was. That gave Caroline an extremely uncomfortable feeling.

'And what about Alex, the husband? We had him in for assaulting Charlie Ford yesterday. Do we know where he went after he was bailed?'

'At the pub. Fully backed up by CCTV and phone track-ing. One of the surveillance team was on him the whole time.'

Caroline shook her head. The last thing Alex Lawson needed was to be drinking. He'd already spent the week suspected of murder, then being arrested and bailed for assaulting Charlie Ford. She wasn't entirely sure adding alcohol to his clearly rage-fuelled mix was going to help him any.

In the corner of the room, a phone rang. Aidan picked it up, then relayed the news to Caroline.

'Update from the hospital. They've finished with Sophie Lawson. We can speak to her.'

55

Caroline had seen enough of hospitals lately. Still, she was thankful to be visiting one on a work call rather than having to be here for her own health reasons.

En route to the hospital, Dexter received a call from Sara Henshaw, who had an update on Alex Lawson. Sophie had specifically asked the police and paramedics not to contact Alex last night, saying they'd had a disagreement and she didn't want him there. By the morning, though, she'd changed her mind. Officers had gone round to his house early that day to let him know his wife had been injured, but he'd already left for work.

'There's something not right there,' Caroline said. 'He came home from the pub to an empty house, woke up in the morning and his wife still wasn't there, and he didn't think to call her or report her missing? Even if they'd had a fight, that's just bizarre.'

'I know,' Sara replied. 'They caught up with him at work

in the end. Apparently he seemed shocked and asked how she was, but then again maybe he's just a good actor.'

Sophie had been put in a private room, with a police officer sitting on a hard plastic chair outside the door. They weren't going to take any risks when it came to her safety. A nurse informed them Alex was in a waiting room, having been told he couldn't see Sophie until they'd completed some tests. It had been agreed he wouldn't be allowed to see Sophie until she had spoken to the police.

Caroline looked at Sophie, and immediately felt a surge of emotions: sorrow at the state she was in, guilt at her own lack of results having put her here and — most of all — intense anger at the person who was doing this. Although there were times when she wanted to jack it all in and give up, she couldn't shake her inbuilt drive for justice. Too many times, she'd seen justice fail. She had to do all she could to make sure it succeeded now.

'How do you feel?' Caroline asked.

'About as good as I look, I imagine.'

'What do you remember?'

Sophie looked off into the distance. 'Nothing much.'

'It's okay. Take your time. Don't stress yourself too much over it. Only tell us what you definitely remember.'

Sophie thought for a moment. 'I was at Mum's. She did dinner. I'd needed a bit of space and a change of scenery.' She shuffled in her bed slightly. 'Christ that hurts.'

'It's okay. Probably best you try to keep still.'

'That's no more comfortable, trust me. I'm fine, but these beds are absolute agony.'

Caroline thought back to the births of Josh and Archie,

and wondered if generic hospital beds had got any better since. She recalled telling the doctors and midwives she was going home that day whether they liked it or not, because she couldn't bear to spend another hour in the place, never mind a whole night. 'I can only imagine,' she said. 'Hopefully you'll be able to leave soon.' As she said this, she wondered how wise it was. Sophie Lawson was far safer in this hospital room with her own private security sitting outside than she would be at home — especially if it turned out her husband was the killer.

'Was it him?' Sophie asked.

'Who?'

'Whoever's been doing this... these things. The one who got Tom, Guy and Megan.'

'We don't know,' Caroline said. 'But we think there's a distinct possibility.'

'But why the car? I thought he did hangings.'

'These are all things we're exploring as a team. But between you and me, killers do sometimes change their methods or do things differently if they think they might get caught.'

Caroline had to tread carefully. She couldn't tell Sophie she and the rest of the group were under surveillance. The likelihood of that getting back to Alex, who was one of their strongest suspects, was too high. Even if Sophie didn't tell him directly, she'd unavoidably change her behaviour or act differently, which could tip him off. And they still couldn't discount the possibility that Sophie herself was either the killer or heavily involved with him. Their killer was clever — that much they knew — and it wasn't beyond the wit of man to assume that he or she might throw in some diversionary tactics or red herrings to throw them off the scent.

'Did you see the car?' Caroline asked.

Sophie shook her head slowly, then winced in pain. 'Only at the last minute. It didn't have its headlights on. I saw that much.'

'Did you see who was driving?'

'No.'

'Okay. We have a make and model, and there are officers out searching as we speak.'

'Have you told Alex?'

Caroline swallowed. 'He knows what happened, yes.'

'Is he here?'

'He's in the hospital. In a waiting room.'

'Can I... Has he seen me?'

'No. Not yet.'

'Why not? I told the other officer I changed my mind.'

Caroline looked over at Dexter. Sophie would be well aware that it was normal for family to be able to attend a loved one's bedside, but it wasn't their business to tell her they suspected him of being involved in her 'accident'.

'They've been doing all sorts of tests, scans, things like that,' she said. 'You needed rest. We'll make sure he's allowed in as soon as we've gone.'

Sophie seemed to accept this. 'Okay,' she said, her voice a little weak. 'And then what happens?'

Caroline looked at Dexter again, but it was clear neither of them knew the answer.

56

Caroline and Dexter had left the hospital knowing they had to leave the surveillance and safety of Sophie, Alex and Charlie up to EMSOU's specialist team. After all, that's what they were there for, and the Rutland officers had to focus on the job in hand: identifying and apprehending the person who'd killed Tom Medland, Guy Sherman and Megan Wilkes, and tried to kill Sophie Lawson.

Caroline looked at her watch as she waited outside the council offices on Catmos Street, where they'd arranged to hold the press conference. She couldn't believe it was barely eleven o'clock in the morning. She shuddered as she thought what the next few hours might bring.

Flanked by Chief Superintendent Derek Arnold, Caroline walked into the council chamber and sat down behind the top table, tall banners displaying the Rutland Police insignia standing behind them as Arnold introduced them both and began the press conference.

'Thank you all for attending today,' he said. 'I'm sure you

can appreciate this is a highly unusual situation for Rutland Police, so I thank you in advance for your patience and understanding. I know many of you have been anxious for information after a recent series of seemingly connected deaths in the county. First of all, I'm sure I speak on behalf of the whole of Rutland Police when I say that our thoughts are with the families of those affected. As Chief Superintendent, I have full faith in Detective Inspector Caroline Hills and her team, who have been working around the clock on this case, and who have been making excellent progress. Caroline.'

At the sound of her name, a jolt of adrenaline coursed through her, and she began to speak with a slight tremor in her voice, careful to stick to the plan they'd drawn up. 'Thank you, sir. As the Chief Superintendent just said, our thoughts are very much with the families of those affected, and that is what drives us to ensure justice is done. There has been some speculation as to the identities of people who've died recently, as well as rumours and conjecture as to what happened. Today, we hope to clear that up, set the record straight and ask the public for their help.

'In the past week, there have been three deaths in Rutland. Early last Monday morning, the body of Thomas Medland was discovered in Manton. Two days later, on Wednesday morning, the body of Guy Sherman was discovered at a building site near Lyndon. And on Saturday morning, the body of Megan Wilkes was discovered in woodland between Oakham and Braunston. Thomas, Guy and Megan all knew each other. They went to the same school, and although their lives had sometimes gone separate ways and all were busy people, had kept in touch since, meeting up a few times a year for a meal and drinks. There are aspects of their deaths which concern us, and which we are looking into.

'On the night Thomas Medland died, he'd been drinking with a friend in Oakham. We know he left the Wheatsheaf shortly after ten o'clock, Sunday closing time, and his body was discovered in the early hours of the next morning, Monday, in Manton. We need to trace his movements between those times. We're particularly keen to speak to the owner of a Vauxhall Corsa, which we believe was fitted with false plates.'

Caroline continued for a further ten minutes, detailing what they knew and what they still needed to know. She ended with a plea for any information from anyone who might have overheard a conversation or noticed something that didn't seem right at any point recently. She was keen to point out that the police were happy to filter out what might or might not be useful, and that any local residents should feel comfortable coming forward with anything they might have.

When she'd finished, Derek Arnold opened the room to questions.

The first hand to shoot up was that of a local radio presenter, who'd arrived at the press conference after finishing his breakfast show. Caroline glanced over at Leah MacGregor from the Mercury, but she sat silently, giving nothing away. Caroline nodded at the radio presenter.

'Rob Persani, Rutland Radio. Detective Inspector, do the people of Rutland have anything to worry about?'

'I don't think so, Rob, no. It's our belief that there's no danger to the wider public as a whole.'

'Are you saying that these three people weren't killed by the same person, then?'

'We're working on a number of hypotheses at the moment, but none of them present a wider risk to the general public.'

Not wanting to get cornered on a particular subject, Caroline moved on to another member of the press.

'Darren Greenwood, Oakham Nub News. When you say you believe the three deaths were connected in some way, can you tell us how?'

'Uh, yes. The manner in which they died was similar, although we don't intend to release any details on that out of respect for their families, and because we don't believe it will provide any benefit to the investigation or the plea for public assistance.'

Caroline had noticed that Leah MacGregor from the Rutland and Stamford Mercury had kept quiet so far, which worried her — particularly as MacGregor had been so keen to get information out of Caroline over the weekend. When her hand finally went up, Caroline knew she was in for a rough ride.

'Leah MacGregor, Rutland and Stamford Mercury. Detective Inspector Hills, is there a serial killer on the loose in Rutland?'

Caroline had anticipated this question, but she still found it hard to conceal her reaction to it.

'As we've said,' Arnold interrupted, 'the team are working on a number of hypotheses right now. We don't think it'd do anyone any good to speculate any more widely than that.'

'And is that one of the hypotheses you're working on?' MacGregor asked, staring intently at Caroline.

'It's important we keep a wide range of possibilities in mind when conducting investigations, Leah,' Arnold said. 'It doesn't mean we're actively favouring one theory or avenue over another, nor should anyone draw undue concern from any particular one, but of course we are well aware that were it to transpire that the same person was responsible for three deaths over a period of time, by definition that is what it would be. But, as I say, it's one of many possible explanations, and I certainly don't advise it being publicised as the main focus of the investigation, no matter how tantalisingly salacious it may be for online clicks.'

Caroline managed not to beam as Arnold finished his response, full of admiration for the way he'd handled it and the way he'd turned it round on a sixpence. As the press conference closed, she felt exhausted but energised, hopeful it would either lead to some new information, or potentially even force the killer's hand.

57

Too often, investigations could get clouded by not knowing which way to turn. That was one of the reasons why officers tended to have defined roles and systems in place to ensure the correct organisation of information. And when they hit a sticking point, Caroline liked to get back to basics.

She and Dexter sat in her office, attempting to chart a path through what they knew.

'The link can't just be that they were all friends,' Caroline said. 'It's *a* link, but it can't be *the* link. It's not reason enough for murder. There has to be something else that links them. Maybe them being old friends was what led to this other connection.'

'I still think it goes back further,' Dexter said.

'You read too much history.'

'No, seriously. A few things make me think this has been lined up for a while. Look at how carefully it's all been done. We've not been able to get close to him. If it weren't for a couple of slip-ups with Tom Medland, we probably wouldn't have got this far. Alright, there were issues with Megan's death too, but maybe he got desperate. Either way, he's got this far without us being able to nail him. You know as well as I do that most murders aren't massively premeditated, and that means the killers make mistakes and are caught easily. This guy's one step ahead of us at all stages. That tells me the murders *were* massively premeditated. So, he's been planning it for a while. We know that much. Let's look at the group of friends. Guy Sherman had been living down in Bristol, but he came back to Rutland after being offered a lucrative job as an architect for a local businessman. Alex and Sophie Lawson were thinking of moving away for better jobs, but then — what do you know — Alex gets offered a great job on a massive salary in Stamford, right on the edge of Rutland.'

'Bloody hell, Dex. I hadn't even noticed that. But you're right.'

Caroline opened her office door and assembled her small team for an emergency briefing.

'Okay, guys. It's time for a change in strategy. We've been too focussed on looking at forensics, CCTV, all that stuff. Our man is clever. Too clever. He knows all that stuff, and that isn't where he's going to slip up. Even when we think he *has* slipped up, he's one step ahead. We think he was daft enough to leave tyre tracks, reckon we're clever by identifying the exact car that did it, find a matching reg number, turns out he's cloned the plates in order to frame someone else. We're not in charge here. He is. He's been leading us the whole way, and that's why we've not been able to touch him. If we keep doing what we're doing, we'll always be at least one step behind. So we need a new angle.

'He's been planning this a long time. Years, probably. And for all we know, Tom Medland might not have been the first. Dex, you like your history. I need you to delve deeper into suicides in the Rutland area. Hangings in particular, but let's not limit ourselves. Aidan, Sara, I need you to massively branch out on the social circles and connections of our victims. There's someone or something we're missing. There's a reason we've been focusing on Charlie Ford and the Lawsons. It's because that's exactly where he wants us to focus. We need to look at patterns of behaviour over the past few years. We know some of the group moved away or thought about moving away, but they either came back or stayed here. I know it's hard, but we need to ignore what's been put in front of us and look behind the scenes. That's where we'll find our answer.'

As Caroline finished speaking, she realised the impact of what she'd just said, and the severity of the complete change of strategy. Although she felt sure in her gut she was right, she hoped for her sake, as well as her team's, that she was.

58

Sophie's leg was agony and her arm felt like it'd been hit with a sledgehammer, but they were nothing compared to the irritation caused by the pain in the arse sitting next to her.

She didn't know whether to feel annoyed or distressed at Alex being there, but the fact she didn't feel comforted or reassured told her a lot. Whichever way things went next, their marriage was over. She was tired of hanging off his arm like a piece of jewellery, sick of listening to him gloat and brag about his brilliant job and all the money he was making. The only people who preened and pointed at their piles of cash were those who knew they hadn't really earned it, or who were scared of losing the lot. He reminded her of the lottery winners she saw in the papers, who happily patted themselves on the back with a smug grin at having drawn a small black smudge over six numbers. They were inevitably the same people who six months later were driving around in Range Rovers, a Rolex hanging off their wrist and swigging Bollinger like it was going out of fashion.

She thought back to her dad. She missed him. He taught her more about life than anyone else, and when she looked back now she realised he was — in his own way — warning her to keep an eye on Alex. Although Alex liked to think he was a lover of fine things, he knew nothing compared to her dad. He'd been a keen enthusiast and collector of watches and pens, as well as a few other items. They must be worth a fortune now, but there was no way her mum would ever part with them. She was more than happy living in her three-bed detached house and keeping his memory alive through his collections.

Sophie remembered him telling her once there was a reason why most people thought Rolex made the best watches and Mont Blanc made the best fountain pens. 'It's so you can spot a dickhead a mile off,' he used to say, before explaining why no serious watch enthusiast rated the Rolex brand. 'A man with a Rolex follows. A man with a Patek Philippe leads.'

It wasn't just glitzy watch brands that irked him, either. Having worked in the motor trade all his life, he was only too keen to point out that some of the most 'desirable' cars were also the worst engineered. 'You can buy a car or you can buy a badge,' was another of his favourite sayings. Despite his wealth and nous, he'd spent his life driving Saabs, Volvos and Volkswagens, telling her that people in Mercedes, BMWs and other premium brands had 'bought an advert'.

She'd chuckled at his lines and his ways back then, but now she'd come to realise not only was he right, but that he'd seen all of those foibles in Alex. And as her husband sat next to her in her hospital bed, she could do nothing but pity him and feel sorry for him.

'Didn't you wonder where I was?' she asked, feeling a sudden rise in her own power.

'What do you mean?'

'It's eleven o'clock in the morning. I've been here since last night. Didn't it even occur to you where I was?'

Alex shrugged. 'I thought you'd stayed at your mum's.'

'You didn't know that, though. For all you knew I could've been involved in an accident on the way home. And as luck would have it, you wouldn't've been far off. Why didn't you even call or text to find out where I was?'

'Like I said, I thought you were at your mum's.'

'What, and you got up this morning, saw I still wasn't there and just went to work as if nothing had happened?'

'Come on, Soph. We've hardly been close recently, have we? I thought you were in a mood with me again and had gone to stay at your mum's. I didn't think ringing you up and seeing if you wanted me to hang around for breakfast was the brightest idea. How was I supposed to know something like this would happen?'

'Oh, I don't know, Alex. Common sense? And do you think there might be a reason why we haven't been close?'

'I dunno. Presumed it was your time of the month.'

'Or maybe because you put your hand against my throat and pinned me against the bloody wall.'

'Alright, keep your voice down.'

'Why? Afraid someone might find out what you're like? Well wouldn't that be a massive shame. I'd hate to damage your fragile little ego.'

'Jesus, Soph. What's got into you? You've changed.'

'No, I've woken up. Everything that's happened recently has made me realise a lot of things.'

'You're scared, aren't you?'

'Scared? Of you?'

'No. The murders. It's alright. We're all worried. Especially after seeing how badly the police are handling it.'

'What a surprise, the man who's just been released from custody is the one slagging off the police.'

'Alright, so who did this then, eh? Who ran you over in the darkness and sped off? Just some random passer-by? You know it's him, Soph. We both know it's Charlie.'

'And why would Charlie want to do any of that? I don't like the guy, but he's not a killer. Anyway, I thought you two were close. Why have you suddenly jumped back and started pointing the finger at him? Sounds like the actions of a guilty man to me.' She watched as Alex stood up. 'What? Going to pin me against the wall again, are you?'

'If you're so sure Charlie's innocent, Soph, that only leaves one explanation.'

'Come on then, Sherlock.'

'Well I know I didn't kill anyone. That just leaves you.'

Sophie laughed, feeling the pain in her ribs as Alex scowled at her reaction. The door opened and the doctor entered, smiling.

'How are you feeling, Sophie?'

'Bruised. But fine.'

'On the plus side, it looks like bruises are the worst of it. We're happy to discharge you and let you get home. You've been a lucky lady.'

'I'll bring the car round,' Alex said.

'No you won't,' Sophie replied. 'You need to get back to work. I'll call Mum. She can pick me up.'

59

Later that afternoon, Dexter came into Caroline's office with a notebook and a stack of printed papers.

'Alright,' he said, 'I've been going through the records looking for any evidence that Tom Medland might not have been the first victim. I'll be honest, there's nothing that seems to fit the bill. Even in the past five years there's only been a tiny handful of suicides in the county, and none with any connection to Tom Medland, Guy Sherman or Megan Wilkes, so far as I can tell. These are the names,' he said, passing a sheet of paper to Caroline. 'I've done what I can in looking at things like ages, backgrounds, schooling, employment records. No patterns I can make out at all, and no connections with our victims. In fact, we've got to go back eighteen years before there's even anyone who went to the same school at about the same time. Kid called Simon Butler. He would've been the year below most of our group, but no other connections that I can see.'

'What happened to him?' Caroline asked.

'His family moved to Scotland shortly after. New start, I imagine.'

'No, I mean the way he died.'

'Hanging. Definitely suicide, though. Poor lad was only fourteen. He left a note and had been talking to a friend on MSN Messenger — remember that? — earlier that day, telling her how he'd been bullied, felt depressed and was thinking of ending it all. Plus his family were all in the house and no-one else went in or out. Pretty open and shut case, that one.'

'Right. We can probably discount that, then.'

'Unless it's the suicide cult thing.'

'What, so a random kid in their school kills himself, then they all wait the best part of twenty years then pop themselves off one by one in the space of a week? Doesn't quite add up to me.'

'Well no, obviously we know they didn't kill themselves, but what if someone's, like... I dunno, completing the circle or something?'

'But twenty years later?'

'Yeah. I know. Just riffing. Got to look at all angles, really.'

'What about the others? How are they getting on looking at wider social circles for our victims?'

'Alright, I think. I haven't heard Aidan shouting "Eureka" yet, so presumably they haven't found anything of interest. To be honest, I've had my head stuck in this all day. But I get the impression they're onto something. Sara's been burrowed in her computer for ages, and she's got that tunnel vision look about her.'

'Alright, well, fingers crossed. And how've you been?' she asked him, changing the tone of her voice.

'How d'you mean?'

'Well, we've not really had a chance to catch up or chat recently. I just wondered how you were getting on.'

'Alright, I think.'

'Good. Between you and me, I think we've built a cracking little team here, and I'm really excited about what lies ahead of us. I see you as a major part of that.'

Dexter shifted his weight to the other foot and rubbed his chin.

'What's the matter, Dex?'

'Eh? Oh, nothing.'

'You sure? You don't exactly look too excited at the prospect.'

'It's alright. We'll have a proper meeting once this is all over with.'

'A meeting? Dex, what's up? You can tell me.'

'Honestly, it's fine. I shouldn't have said anything.'

'You haven't. That's the problem.'

Dexter took a deep breath, then sighed. 'I've just been thinking about my future, that's all. Trying to plan ahead and work out what I want to do.'

'How do you mean? You thinking of a career change?'

'I dunno. Sort of. Maybe.'

'Is this about your parents?' Caroline asked, knowing Dexter's mum and dad had been pushing him as a child to be a doctor, and that he'd chosen the police force as something of an ironic rebellion.

'No, no. I'm not going to med school, if that's what you think. Just trying to work out what I want, you know? I'm at that stage in my life.'

'Think yourself lucky you're not worrying about hot flushes. The worst thing you men get at "that stage of life" is a penchant for buying sports cars.'

Dexter laughed. 'I'm not at that stage yet, thank god. Although I am looking forward to picking up scantily-clad young women in my Porsche.'

Caroline smiled. 'Let's sit down and have a chat over a beer or two once this has all blown over, alright? It'd be unprofessional of me to try and talk you out of anything, but I'm totally going to try and talk you out of it.'

Before Dexter could think of a witty response, there was a knock at Caroline's office door and Sara Henshaw entered.

'Guv,' she said, a clear and serious look on her face. 'You need to come through. I think we might have something.'

60

'Okay, so we've been going through the backgrounds of our victims in more detail, like you asked,' Sara said, sitting down at her desk as Caroline and Dexter crowded round. Aidan perched on the edge of his own desk, already sternly aware of what he and Sara had uncovered.

'Hit me with it,' Caroline said, feeling a shift in the atmosphere that told her they were close to catching their killer.

'We didn't quite have all the pieces joined up until Dexter gave us the list of suicides he just brought through to you. It wasn't until we had everything in one place that we worked it out.'

'Sara, please tell me.'

'Sorry. It's a little bitty, but it all makes sense once it comes together. So, let's start with Guy Sherman. He'd moved to Bristol for university and set up a new life there, but came back to Rutland after getting a job offer to be the architect on the new spa resort near Lyndon, and being promised lots of well-paid work. We know that Alex and Sophie Lawson had planned to move away, but then Alex got offered a lucrative job at an advertising agency in Stamford, which kept them in the area. His salary, by the way, is nearly double the average for that sort of job. Sticks out like a sore thumb once you look at it in context. Aidan dug a little further and looked into the companies that employed Guy Sherman and Alex Lawson. The leisure group that's building the new spa hotel complex is, as we know, headed by Owen Samuels. The advertising agency Alex Lawson works for is a bit trickier. That's owned by a shell company, but we've managed to trace it back to the ultimate owner. They bought the agency out not long before they offered Alex the job. The owner is a guy by the name of Gareth Butler. It was Dexter's list of names that set us off on the right line. One of the first ones he mentioned was a four-teen-year-old called Simon Butler, who took his own life about twenty years ago.'

'The one who was in the school year below our victims?'

'The year below most of them, yeah. I thought, well, Butler isn't the rarest name in the world, but it's worth looking into, just in case there's a link. So I looked back at the case notes and news reports from the time. Turns out Simon had a brother called — guess what?'

'I'll have a tenner on Gareth,' Dexter said.

'Got it in one.'

Caroline massaged her brow. 'Okay, so the brother of a boy who took his own life twenty years ago is now Alex Lawson's boss, right?'

'Right,' Sara said. 'Just a coincidence, perhaps. But then we looked at the group's living arrangements. The land that Charlie Ford lives on is registered to Gareth Butler too. So we dug a bit deeper, tried to find out where he lived, see if we could come up with anything of interest. Turns out the last known address for Gareth Butler is where Owen Samuels now lives. However, there's no record of a sale having taken place at any time. Bit odd, especially as we know Owen Samuels lives alone, but Aidan had a hunch. So we looked up Owen Samuels. He only appears on the scene fairly recently. We reckon Gareth Butler changed his name to Owen Samuels by deed poll. They're the same person.'

'But wouldn't there be some record of that? Can we confirm it?' Caroline asked.

'We can, but not easily. Contrary to popular belief, there's no official deed poll office. To change your name, all you actually need to do is show you've changed it in good faith, have publicly assumed your new name and that there's no fraudulent reason for doing so. All you need is a solicitor to prepare and sign the paperwork and you're done.'

'Jesus. So we need to find the solicitor?'

'We're working on it. But look at the evidence. Gareth Butler's brother hangs himself at the age of fourteen, having expressed a desire to end his life because of bullying at school. Gareth Butler then buys out the company that employs Alex Lawson. He's also, we assume, the same person as Owen Samuels, who employed Guy Sherman, ensuring the whole group is kept in one place. Then they start dying, one by one, by hangings that're made to look like suicide.'

Caroline could feel her heart thumping in her chest. Her scalp began to itch, as it often did at times of high stress. 'Bloody hell. Okay, let's think about this. We spoke to Owen Samuels after Guy Sherman died. We haven't come across Gareth Butler before, have we?'

'No, guv.'

'But presumably Alex Lawson will have done, seeing as Butler's his employer. Get hold of Alex. We need a description of Gareth Butler. As detailed as possible. If he can get Butler somewhere for a chat or something, even better. Then surveillance from EMSOU can confirm if it's the same person and we can arrest. Aidan, can you get onto them now and find out where Alex is?'

'Will do,' Aidan said, as Dexter dialled Alex Lawson's number on his desk phone, handing the receiver over to Caroline.

She waited and waited, listening to the ringing tone, before the call eventually patched through to Alex's voicemail.

'Bugger. Redial, Dex.'

Caroline clenched her jaw as she listened to the ringing tone over and over again, before putting down the phone and slumping into a chair.

A few moments later, Aidan's phone rang. He mumbled a few words, looked over at Caroline, then put the phone down.

'That was them. Alex Lawson's at work. He received a call from the office number about twenty minutes ago and headed straight in.'

'Christ,' Caroline said.

'Guv?' Sara said, interrupting her. 'Just a thought, but it might be wise to call for backup. If Gareth Butler, Owen

Samuels, whatever we're calling him is on the premises, Alex's life could be in immediate danger.'

'It gets worse,' Aidan said. 'Alex's phone sent a text to Sophie's phone a minute ago, asking Sophie to meet him at the office.'

61

Caroline's Volvo bumped out onto Station Road and accelerated away, Dexter beside her in the passenger seat. She'd told
Aidan to get a message to the surveillance officers to keep their
distance from Sophie, so as not to spook Gareth Butler. The
last thing they wanted was for him to realise they were on to
him and either kill Alex — if it wasn't already too late — or
take drastic measures on himself.

Caroline was sure that message hadn't been sent by Alex,
but by Gareth himself. And that meant Sophie was next.

Heading in on their own was a huge risk, and the potential
fallout either way could be catastrophic. The instinctively
logical move would be to get local officers to the scene as
quickly as possible. Lincolnshire Police had a station in the
centre of Stamford, and officers from there could be on the
scene within minutes. But the situation was far more delicate
than that. With the time it'd take them to call through to
Lincolnshire, explain the situation and have officers briefed

and dispatched, Caroline had taken the snap judgement that it'd be just as quick to go themselves.

By the time Sophie had read the text, got ready, and arrived at the office, Caroline reckoned they could just about beat her to it. Dexter was busily checking the distances on Google Maps as Caroline sped down the A606 and along the north shore of Rutland Water.

'Depends on traffic,' he said, 'but it's probably a five or six minute drive into town for her. Then she's got to get parked and walk to the office.'

'What if she's walking the whole way?' Caroline asked.

Dexter tapped an icon on his phone screen. 'This reckons twenty minutes. If she left as soon as she got the text and has driven in, she might just get there first. If she's taken a bit longer to read it or get her shoes on, we might have the edge. If she's walking, we'll definitely be alright.'

Caroline clenched her jaw as she overtook a line of traffic just outside Whitwell. She didn't know what awaited her in Stamford, but she knew it wouldn't be a plate of biscuits and a hot cup of tea.

As a trained crisis negotiator, she already had a slight advantage. But she doubted whether the same strategies would work on a man who'd already killed at least three people and had been planning their murders for years.

As they reached the outskirts of Stamford, Caroline kept her eyes on the road ahead. She needed to reach the offices of Charnley & Walker as quickly as possible, but getting there in one piece was crucial.

When they finally arrived in the town centre, Caroline parked the car next to All Saints Church, knowing she'd likely come back to a parking ticket, but with that being far from the most worrying thing on her mind. She and Dexter jogged over the road to the offices of Charnley & Walker, and Caroline opened the door.

'Where is it?' she asked, panting even though they'd only jogged a couple of dozen yards.

'Got to be up there,' Dexter said, pointing to a staircase.

Caroline took the stairs two at a time, feeling her legs burning with the first real physical exertion she'd done in a long time. When they reached the top, she pushed open the door to the Charnley & Walker office and stood aghast at the sight in front of her.

62

The man they'd known as Owen Samuels stood propped against the back wall, a sardonic smile crossing his face.

'Oh dear,' he said, his voice calm. 'Too clever for my own good.'

Barely four or five feet in front of him, Alex Lawson stood on a wheeled office chair, his hands taped together, a piece of fabric stuffed in his mouth and a noose around his neck. Although he was trembling slightly, he seemed to be well aware that one wrong movement would send the chair skittering along the hardwood floor, hanging him in the process.

'I wouldn't come any closer,' Owen said.

'It's okay. We're staying right here,' Caroline said, feeling rivulets of sweat starting to trickle down her back. 'Is Sophie here too?'

'No. I thought you were her arriving. She'll be here any minute,' Owen said, speaking with the composed and unruffled voice of a front-desk receptionist.

'Then what?'

'Then she watches her husband die. As do you, unfortunately. I hadn't planned it to be a spectator sport, but that's what you get for gatecrashing.'

The sound of Dexter's phone reverberated off the cold brick walls as the chair Alex was standing on moved slightly, leaving him with a look of sheer panic on his face. Caroline made eye contact with him, willing him to calm down and stay still.

'Don't you dare answer that,' Owen said. 'Put it on the desk over there. You too,' he added, looking at Caroline.

Caroline took her phone out of her pocket and held it for a moment, before carrying it in two hands, walking slowly towards the desk Owen had pointed at. 'Let's stay calm, okay?' she said, placing the phone down gently. 'We don't want any sudden movements or surprises.'

'We certainly don't. The main prize today is making sure Sophie sees this.'

'What's she done, Owen?' Caroline asked.

'It's more what she didn't do that's the problem. She's complicit.'

'In what?'

'You'll find out sooner or later, I'm sure.'

'Is this about Simon?'

Owen Samuels's eyes locked with hers, and for the first time she saw something behind that dispassionate, if slightly icy stare. It was there for barely a second, though — a quick glimpse under the veil at Gareth Butler — before the level-headed Owen returned. 'You know nothing,' he said.

'I know you want to see the whole group suffer and die,' Caroline replied. 'Tom, Guy, Megan. Now Alex, Sophie and Charlie. I just want to understand why. Can you tell me?'

'I can tell you I won't get to see Charlie suffer or die, unfortunately. Although if you open the window and listen very carefully in about... fifteen minutes,' he said, looking at his watch, 'you might even hear it from here.'

'Hear what?'

'The explosion. The farm's barely a mile or two away as the crow flies.' Owen reached his hand out to the side and unlatched the window, pushing it open without taking his eyes off Caroline or Dexter. 'Smell that? Beautiful fresh air. South-westerly winds, too, if I'm not mistaken. We might even be able to smell him.'

'Are you saying there's going to be an explosion at the farm where Charlie Ford lives? What sort of explosion?'

'Oh, come on. As if I'm going to tell you that. It's bad enough not being able to watch him die. At least give me the pleasure of knowing it's happened.'

'Why an explosion for Charlie? Why not the same as the others?'

'Unfortunately, that one's your fault. Let's call it an insurance policy. Just in case I wasn't able to get out of here after this and see to him myself.'

'A dead man's switch?' Caroline asked. 'That's very clever.'

'Thank you.'

'How does it work?'

Owen laughed again. 'Seriously, I know the score, Inspector. Give me some credit.'

'Trust me, I give you a huge amount of credit. You've been

one step ahead of us the whole way. I'm just genuinely interested.'

'Oh well, if you must know. GSM,' he said, taking a mobile phone out of his pocket and holding it in front of him. 'There's a phone attached to a circuit at the farm. If I ring the number before the pre-set time, it'll break the circuit and stop the detonation. But if I don't call the number... Well, let's just say bits of Charlie will be scattered far and wide. A bit like this.'

Before Caroline or Dexter could react, Owen tossed the phone out of the open window, watching them as they heard it smash to smithereens on the road below.

Owen smiled. 'Whoops. How careless of me. Don't worry, though. I won't drop this,' he said, pulling a large hunting knife from the back of his belt.

Caroline looked at Dexter, seeing a look of panic and desperation on his face. She knew what was going through his mind. Charlie Ford's death warrant had just been signed, and there was nothing they could do about it. If they reached for their phones to raise the alarm, Owen would simply flick out a leg to kick the chair Alex was standing on, killing him instantly. Armed with the knife, he'd likely inflict heavy damage on Caroline and Dexter, too, if not worse. If they moved, it was over for Alex. But if they waited, Charlie Ford would be scattered across southern Rutland and Sophie Lawson would see her own husband murdered in front of her, before likely being killed herself. If Owen had been clever enough to plan a dead man's switch as an insurance policy for Charlie, what was to say he hadn't done the same for Sophie?

Yet again, Owen Samuels had been one step ahead of them all.

'It's alright, Dex,' Caroline said. 'It'll be okay.'

Just as she hoped her words might have at least gone some tiny way to putting her colleague's mind at ease, they heard the noise of a door opening downstairs.

63

Sophie Lawson stepped into the room, a look of sheer terror on her face.

'What's going on? Who are you? What have you done to him?' she asked, panic rising in her voice.

'One question at a time, Sophie,' Owen replied. 'To answer your first, I'm pretty sure you can see exactly what's going on. You never had any trouble with that. Your only problem was having the guts to do anything about it. To your second question, I'm not surprised you haven't worked that one out either. But, to be honest, that just goes to prove you never did give a shit.' For the first time, Caroline could hear real venom beginning to creep into Owen's voice. 'And to answer your third, nothing. Yet.'

'Let him go! Get him down! Why are you doing this?'

'Really, Sophie, you must calm down. You didn't get this excited when Alex and his friends were throwing eggs at Simon, did you? Or when they tied him to the gym apparatus.'

'What? What the hell are you talking about?'

'It's okay, Sophie. Stay calm,' Caroline said.

'No, I didn't think you'd remember. Just another day for people like you, isn't it? People who don't give a toss about others. But actions have consequences, Sophie. And sometimes the people taking those actions don't even realise what they are. It might not even register on their radar. But somewhere, deep down, what they're actually doing is killing somebody.'

'You're crazy. Who are you?'

Owen rolled his eyes and gave a snort of derision. 'Enough.'

Before any of them could realise what was happening, Owen kicked the chair from under Alex, and lunged at Sophie with the knife.

64

Their reactions were purely instinctive more than anything. Dexter acted first, spotting the immediate danger and throwing himself at Owen, tackling him to the floor as the knife sliced the air in front of Sophie's face. Caroline struggled to hold the weight of Alex, trying desperately to lift him and reduce the effect of the noose on his neck, not knowing whether the trembling and jerking was from her own muscular exertions or the last spasms of a dying man.

Alex's weight was too much for her even if she was fighting fit, but in her weakened state she knew she couldn't hold on any longer.

'Dex... Please...' she grunted, watching as her colleague fought to pin down Owen Samuels. For a brief moment, she thought Owen had overpowered him, but she quickly realised Dexter had let go, freeing his arm so he could pummel a fist into the side of Owen's face. She felt the burning in her arms and back as she struggled to keep Alex's weight off the noose, not knowing whether the man above her was dead or alive, or what would happen to any of them. In the corner of the room, Sophie stood shaking and screaming.

Caroline tried to force the words out, but all her strength was going into holding Alex up as best she could. 'Sophie. Help me.'

The words seemed to get through to her, and after a second Sophie rushed over and took on some of Alex's weight.

'Have you got him?' Caroline asked. 'I need to untie the rope.'

'No. No, I can't take his weight. Don't move. Please!'

Before Caroline could reply, she heard the low and distant boom of an explosion.

65

For the second time that week, Caroline found herself heading to the hospital to visit a Lawson.

'Ah, his friend and saviour,' the doctor said as Caroline introduced herself ahead of seeing Alex.

'Well, I wouldn't go that far.'

'I mean it quite literally. His vitals are good. We're awaiting the results of a brain scan, but we've no indication that'll be anything other than normal. If so, that'll be thanks to the quick reactions of you and your colleague. Some of the veins and nerves here in the neck,' the doctor said, pointing to his own, 'don't tend to do very well when force is applied to them. In fact, continued pressure can lead to stagnant hypoxia and loss of consciousness in seconds.'

'So I understand,' Caroline said. 'I always thought it was one of those "only in the movies" things.'

'No, not at all. Just a slight difference in pathophysiology. Most people think the victim's fallen unconscious because of the pressure on their windpipe stopping them breathing, but that'd take a whole lot longer. Nerve compression, hypoxia, goodnight. At that point, the neck muscles relax because the person's unconscious, so additional force can be more easily applied. Then you're looking at complete arterial occlusion, permanent damage to the brain and death. Crushing the windpipe to stop someone breathing is actually incredibly difficult.'

'So he's okay?' Caroline asked, wanting to change the subject to something a little less morbid.

'He's fine. The nurse is running a couple of tests, but you can go in and see him afterwards. How's your colleague?'

Caroline thought back to the immediate aftermath of the showdown with Owen Samuels. The explosives Owen had rigged over time at the farm had gone off a few minutes early. The brief moment of surprise had given Dexter the half-second he needed to gain the upper hand, wrestling the knife out of his hands and pinning him fully to the floor. It was only when backup arrived and things started to calm down that Caroline realised Dexter's arm and hand had been slashed in the struggle.

'He'll be alright,' Caroline said. 'In fact, he wanted me to ask — do you have any Peppa Pig plasters?'

The doctor laughed. 'I'll see what we can do. Shall we?' he said, gesturing towards the door of the room Alex was in.

They stepped inside, and Caroline smiled at Sophie, who returned the gesture with a little less sincerity. 'How's he doing?' she whispered, noticing Alex appeared to be asleep.

'He's fine,' Alex answered, opening his eyes. 'And looking forward to getting out of here. Have you locked the bastard up?' he asked Caroline.

'He's in custody, yes.'

'And what about my job? Who's going to pay me now?'

Caroline shared a look with Sophie. 'I'm sure you'll figure something out,' she said.

There was a knock at the door, and the doctor entered again. 'Sorry — another visitor has just arrived for Alex. I can let him in, but I'm afraid we're only allowed two at a time in here, so one of you will have to step outside for a bit.'

As the doctor finished speaking, Caroline's phone vibrated. 'That'll be me, then,' she said, stepping out and walking a little further down the corridor, watching as Charlie Ford walked into Alex's room.

Caroline'd had to think on her feet, and she was thankful beyond belief that it had worked. When Owen had demanded they put their phones on the table in the office, Caroline realised this could be their last chance to get a message out. She'd glanced down at her phone briefly and unlocked the screen using Face ID, before tapping Sara's name in the call list. As she walked over, she held the volume button down, ensuring everything stayed silent at their end, before putting the phone face-down on the table. That meant Sara had heard everything from that point on, including Owen telling them about the farm explosion. Fortunately, Sara had managed to get the message to Charlie in just enough time for him to get to a safe distance.

Caroline returned the call volume to its previous level as she answered the incoming call.

'Hello?'

'Mrs Hills? It's Maria from the oncology department at Peterborough City Hospital. We noticed you're a little late for your five o'clock appointment with Mr Anand and wanted to check you were on your way.'

Caroline looked at her watch. Ten past five. She'd completely forgotten about the appointment in the midst of everything else that'd been going on. 'Yes,' she said, looking for signs that could direct her to the right area of the hospital. 'In fact, I've literally just got here, so I should be with you in a couple of minutes.'

Spotting a sign that pointed her in the direction of the oncology department, Caroline put her phone back in her pocket and picked up the pace.

66

Caroline sat down in Mr Pankash Anand's consulting room and tried to gauge his body language. As ever, he was keeping his cards close to his chest and relying purely on the words that were to come.

'How have you been?' Mr Anand asked her, looking over the rim of his spectacles.

'Busy,' Caroline replied. 'Healthwise, okay I think. Nausea and vomiting. Tiredness. Lethargy. I've been getting out of breath a lot, too.'

Mr Anand nodded. 'That's quite normal. Your body's putting all of its energy into fighting the cancer, which is good news.'

The inflection of his words concerned Caroline. 'But there's also bad news?' she asked.

'I'd say there's also less than ideal news,' he replied, choosing his words carefully. 'Your most recent scan seems to indicate that the cancer may have progressed to stage two.'

Caroline felt an icy chill down her spine. 'What? No, the

new chemotherapy treatment was meant to shrink it and get rid of it.'

'That's the plan, yes. And it's one we'll stick with as we think that gives you the greatest possible chance of making a full recovery. But the scans show the cancer has spread to the uterus. The good news is at the moment we've not seen it spreading elsewhere, so we're only moving to stage two, but I would be lying if I said it wasn't a cause for concern.'

'What can you do?' she asked, suddenly feeling desperately alone and wishing she had Mark and the boys beside her.

'That's what I wanted to discuss with you today. The chemotherapy does seem to be having an effect on the ovarian cancer itself, which is good. We're actually seeing a small reduction there. The spread of the cancer is a concern, but because so far it seems to have spread only to the uterus, there are options. Personally, my very strong recommendation at this stage would be surgical.'

'Surgical? An operation?'

'Yes,' Mr Anand said. 'My personal recommendation would be a hysterectomy. Removal of the uterus, and potential removal of the Fallopian tubes and ovaries, should that be a viable option at the time of surgery.'

Caroline slowly nodded, feeling a swell of emotions rising inside her.

67

Caroline didn't want to go straight home. She needed Mark and the boys beside her, but more than anything she needed the time to process things in her own mind.

She hadn't needed her sat nav, nor did she need to try and remember the route she'd taken last time she came here. Now, temporarily, there was a very obvious landmark: the plume of smoke that still rose into the sky as the last remnants of the fire were brought under control just outside Tinwell.

'You're too late,' she said to Leah MacGregor as she walked from her car to the cordon around the farm. 'You missed the good bit.'

'I think we all heard the good bit. I was on the scene within fifteen minutes. I've just come back to get an update. Funny, I don't remember seeing you around earlier.'

'I was otherwise engaged.'

'With finding your serial killer, I hope.'

'Yes, actually. We've got someone in custody.'

'A suspect?'

'No, he's coughed. He'll be charged with the murders of Tom Medland, Guy Sherman and Megan Wilkes. There you go, you got your exclusive after all.'

'Any idea what happened here?' MacGregor asked, gesturing towards the devastation in front of them. 'They won't tell me anything. A guy down the road said he'd been told it was a bomb. Al Qaeda, he reckons.'

Caroline laughed. 'In Rutland?'

'I didn't say I believed him.'

'No, but it'll get you some clicks, right?'

'We've got high editorial standards,' MacGregor said, looking mortally offended.

'I know, Leah. I'm joking. In all seriousness, thank you. We do still need the public to get involved and send us any information that might be useful, though.'

MacGregor cocked her head. 'I thought you said he'd admitted it?'

'He has, but that needs to be backed up by evidence. Otherwise a smart brief'll make him stand up in court and claim he was coerced into a confession. You'll be amazed how often that happens.'

'I don't think anything would amaze me anymore. Who'd have thought? All this drama in little old Rutland.'

Caroline nodded. 'Yeah. And to think I came here to get away from it all.'

'Still, all over now, eh? No more dramas.'

'Yeah,' Caroline said, her mind shifting elsewhere. 'Yeah. No more dramas.'

68

Before heading home, Caroline swung by the office to collect her bag and close down her computer for the night. She'd left in such a hurry earlier, she couldn't even remember the state she'd left the place in, although she had a sneaking suspicion Sara would've run a hoover round, switched off the lights and left Caroline's bag by the door. Even a major explosion and the capture of a serial killer wouldn't dampen her enthusiasm or efficiency.

When she arrived, she not only found the lights on, but Dexter was in the office, sitting at his computer.

'Guv. Sorry, didn't think anyone was around.'

'Neither did I. What're you doing here, Dex?'

'I had to come back to get my car. Thought I'd shut the computer down while I was here, but I made the mistake of checking my emails, didn't I?'

'Schoolboy error. How's the hand? Can you drive?'

'Yeah, it's the left one. The car's an auto, so lean over, stick it in Drive, off we go.'

'What about the steering wheel?'

Dexter shrugged. 'One handed.'

'Sounds safe.'

'Well, seeing as you're here, and for the sake of giving my hand an extra hour or two to heal, why don't we grab a drink?'

Caroline's instinct was to say no. She had to get home. She needed to see Mark and the boys and curl up with a large glass of wine and a blanket. But the look on Dexter's face told her it was more a plea than a suggestion.

'ON THE PLUS SIDE, he won't be coming out again,' Dexter said, as they sat down in a corner of The Wheatsheaf in Oakham with two halves of Tiger.

'Probably not, no. We'll be pushing for three whole-life sentences. Especially considering the level of premeditation.'

'And the time! Jesus Christ, he must've been planning it for years.'

'Ever since his brother took his own life, according to his statement,' Caroline replied. 'There are pages and pages, according to Aidan. I'll go through it all in the morning. He knows there's no chance of getting out or getting off, and in any case he wanted everyone to know exactly why he did it.'

'Kind of the whole point, I guess, if he felt he was avenging his brother's death.'

'Yep. The wonderful minds of the deranged. Speaking of which, I hope you're planning on sticking around.'

'Me? Yeah, why wouldn't I be?'

'You mentioned the other day you were thinking about your future.'

'Oh. Yeah. Don't worry about that. That's a conversation for another time.'

'Alright. As long as we're not losing you, Dex. This team needs you. I need you.'

Dexter smiled.

69

Statement provided to Rutland Police by Owen Samuels, also known as Gareth Butler.

THE FIRST THING I want to be very clear about is that none of this would have happened were it not for my brother's death. Simon was the best brother anyone could ask for, and I had to watch him shrink and regress more and more every day due to the relentless bullying and torment he was subjected to. The main ringleaders in this were Charlie Ford and Alex Lawson. Thomas Medland joined in from time to time, and towards the end Guy Sherman — who'd been heavily bullied himself before then — decided his own agony wasn't enough, and that he wanted to pile in on poor Simon too.

The girls were far from blameless. Sophie Matthews, who later became Sophie Lawson, used to stand by and watch. She did nothing at all to stop the boys from making my brother's life hell. Megan Wilkes was much the same, when she was around. The only person she cared about was herself, and she'd let the boys get away with anything if it meant she got a shag out of it.

It was me who found Simon. He used to play music in his room all the time. The second one CD ended, he'd have another one on. That day, he'd been playing *Americana* by The Offspring. I remember the whole album. It's imprinted on my mind. There's a minute of silence after *Pay the Man*, then it kicks back in with a weird Mexican version of *Pretty Fly*. Simon's CD player had a function where he could hold down the Skip button and it'd fast-forward the track a few seconds. He had the timing down to a tee and there'd be barely three or four seconds between the two songs. But, that day, the silence was a full minute. After the mariachi version of *Pretty Fly*, it fell silent again so I waited a minute or two and then knocked on his door. I got no reply, so I went in. And that's when I found him hanging.

There were no names in the note, but I knew. Everyone knew. The school should've done something, but they chose not to. They didn't speak to the group. There was no anti-bullying drive. They simply swept it under the carpet, as if Simon's life had never mattered. They didn't care one jot about him.

My parents couldn't stand watching the other kids grow up, moving on, having the life Simon should've had. We moved to Scotland, where our mother had grown up. Reconnecting with another lost childhood.

Everything changed from the moment Simon died. My

parents were husks of their former selves. I lost my innocence. Simon lost his life.

They say time is a great healer, and that things become more distant and faded as the years move on. I didn't have that luxury. I got angrier with every passing year, every birthday Simon missed, every Christmas with an empty chair at the dining table. A-Level results day. His twenty-first birthday. It was all empty and pointless.

I don't know when I first realised I was going to end their lives in the way they'd ended Simon's. I think I knew from day one that Alex, Charlie, Guy and Tom had to die. Those just seemed to be the accepted facts. I don't know why I didn't immediately lump the girls in with them. Maybe there's an implied innocence there. One they didn't deserve.

There wasn't a particular day I sat down and started planning. It evolved over time, always in the background. After I left school, I lost myself in work. I'd lost so much, all I could focus on was building, creating, adding more to the world. It was all empty, but it focused me and kept my mind on something vaguely positive. I did well from it. I set up a number of businesses, sold a couple for large sums of money and kept others running at a healthy ongoing profit. I tried to fly under the radar as much as possible. I didn't want publicity or attention. I just wanted to build and create as much as I could.

I think somewhere in the background I knew the money would come in useful. They say you can't buy happiness. That's true. But you can buy vengeance. I kept close tabs on the group. I needed to know where they were, what they were doing, what they had planned. So I asked them.

None of them recognised me from school. They wouldn't

have done, I don't suppose. Our paths never directly crossed. But you'd be amazed what people tell random strangers in pubs and cafés if you strike up a conversation. That's how I found out Alex and Sophie were thinking of moving away. I simply started chatting to him. I remember it as clear as day. It was a Thursday night. I knew Alex used to pop into The Hurdler for a few drinks with a work colleague every Thursday. We got chatting. We talked about work, he mentioned he was looking for new opportunities. I got his number, told him I might have something up my sleeve for him.

Buying out Charnley & Walker had been easy enough. They'd been struggling for some time, and the owners were only too keen to bite my hand off when I offered them a cash out. It was going to be a money pit, but that wouldn't matter. After a while I could close the place down and sell off the assets. I calculated I'd still be down a hundred grand or so, but it'd be more than worth it. I said I'd heard good things about Alex and wanted him on board. We created a new position just for him, and a salary he couldn't refuse. He didn't.

Guy had already been in Bristol a few years by that point, and he was living the dream. I knew it'd take a serious amount of money to lure him back here. I'd been thinking about building a spa resort anyway. Even I wouldn't go to the extent of signing a multi-million pound leisure contract just to end some rat's life. He was over the moon when I headhunted him and told him I'd heard good things and wanted him to be the architect. It's amazing how a bit of money and ego stroking can make anyone do whatever you want them to.

In comparison, Tom had been a piece of cake. He'd never

shown any ambition whatsoever. He hadn't even moved away for university, choosing to apply to Leicester and live with his parents. His marriage lasted a little longer than his university degree, though, then he was back living with his mum and dad again. I would call it sad and unfortunate, but I won't. It actually made me quite happy to see him wasting his life like that.

The boys had to go first. They were the ones who'd made Simon's life hell — and ended it — and I couldn't risk taking the easy option of killing the girls first, then getting caught and those three getting away with it. Guy and Alex were easy enough — I'd kill them at work. I could lure them in easily enough and ensure no-one else was around. But they couldn't be the first two to go, because the links would've been too obvious. You'd have found me straight away.

From keeping a close eye on the group, I knew Tom's pub crawls with Charlie Ford tended to see him end up legless, and I knew that would give me the best chance. If he was blind drunk, he wouldn't put up a fight. He was to be number one.

I parked up on Northgate and waited for him. I told him there'd been an incident at the train station and no-one was allowed across the line. I said I was a cab driver, and I'd drop him home for nothing as otherwise he'd have one hell of a walk on his hands. He didn't question it when I headed south out of Oakham, even though heading north and into Barleythorpe via the bypass would've been much quicker. By the time we were on the Uppingham Road, he was snoring.

I parked up just outside Manton, where I'd parked the Corsa. I made the plates up myself at the garage I co-own a couple of Sundays before, when no-one was at work. I probably didn't do the best job of it, but it seems to have kept the police occupied for long enough and ensured everything stayed off the record. I strangled Tom in his sleep. He woke up and squirmed a bit, but by then I'd hit the right spot on his neck and he was gone. It took far less effort than I thought it would. For a moment, it scared me just how easy it is to kill a man.

I drove him to the railway bridge, parked up, put the noose around his neck, wrapped him in some thick plastic sheeting then dragged him down the embankment. I thought he'd be hit by a freight train overnight. There's no way in hell you can stop one of those things at full speed, and I thought it'd obliterate all trace of the strangulation. I didn't know there were engineering works planned. I believe that one small mistake is what led to everything else eventually unravelling. But it took far longer than I thought it would. I knew I had to accelerate my plans.

Guy was by far the easiest. I called him and asked him to come to the site at the end of the day because I had something I wanted to go through with him. One of the most important aspects of the build was the view from the bridal suite, and I told him I wasn't happy with it, and that we should go up and take a look now that the shell of the suite was there. I'd tied the noose to the scaffolding before he came. I'd have to get the timing right, but I was confident. He stood on the edge of the scaffolding, trying to see what I was telling him. He hadn't seen the rope tucked away behind the boarding. I slipped it out as I was talking, then in one move I put the noose over his head and pushed him off the scaffolding. It was so easy. I never expected it to work that well. He just went. Another life snuffed out within seconds. I felt so powerful.

After Alex and Megan were brought in, I realised things could potentially go wrong. They had their own secrets to hide, and by that point they were starting to link the two deaths. Alex couldn't be next, because the workplace connection would be too obvious. Megan had to die, and sooner rather than later.

Spoofing phone numbers is incredibly easy. Thirty seconds on Google and a few dollars in your pocket, and you can call or text anybody from any number and make it appear you're them. So sending a message to Megan and luring her out of her flat seemed as easy as pie. How was I meant to know it'd be the first time in her life she'd turned down a shag? That's when I knew I had to get her out of there, so I phoned her.

I'd been keeping an eye on her for a while. In the traditional sense at first, and then I noticed her flat has its electrical consumer unit in the communal area. I went back a few days later and put a couple of dead fuses in. As luck would have it, I put a leaflet through her door a day earlier, advertising my services as an emergency electrician called Brian Waterman. She took the bait and called me. I made a show of running some tests, then told her she'd need some new light switches and sockets, which I could provide there and then for a very good price. Touch sensors on the switches, too! In reality, these doubled up as cameras, and the sockets contained microphones which enabled me to watch her and listen in on her whenever I wanted. That night, I had to scare her enough to get her out of the flat. It worked. I attacked her and drove her out to the woods, and hanged her in the tree.

After that, I realised the police were watching Alex, Sophie and Charlie. I had to come up with a new plan. Alex was easy enough — I could kill him at work after hours. Stacking explosives at Charlie's farmhouse would ensure only he was killed. The explosives were in the wood store, against the back of the farmhouse. I knew he wouldn't be needing firewood at this time of year, so they'd go undetected until I needed to use them.

That left Sophie. Now I knew the police were watching her, I wouldn't be able to hang her. I couldn't get into the house. I couldn't intercept her en route. But when I knew she was going to her mother's, I drove to Bourne. I saw where she'd parked her car. I spotted the surveillance officers a mile off. I knew the route she'd walk from her mother's house to her car, and I saw the perfect opportunity to run her over and disappear without the officers being able to follow me. My only regret is that I didn't kill her. The car is in an old barn I own out on the Fens. I'd planned to hide out there should the police close in on me.

I knew they would eventually. That's why I had the explosives rigged at Charlie's farm. The dead man's switch meant I could detonate them any time I liked. Then I was onto the last leg of my plan: lure Alex into the office, get him to lure Sophie in, kill Alex in front of her and then kill Sophie, knowing Charlie was being blown to smithereens in the meantime.

After that, it didn't matter if the police caught me. My mission would've been complete. They'd all be gone, and Simon's death would have finally been avenged. I have no regrets over the deaths of Tom Medland, Guy Sherman or Megan Wilkes. My only regret is that I was stopped from killing Alex Lawson, Sophie Lawson and Charlie Ford too. I realise my lack of remorse will not stand me in good stead when this case comes before a judge, but I've had enough of lies. I've had enough of deception. The truth is I am not sorry, and I never will be.

Caroline closed the front door behind her, glad to shut the world outside. She wasn't sure what time it was. She couldn't even be certain of the day. All she knew was that she needed to down a glass of wine and head to bed. She was beyond exhausted, in every sense of the word.

'Hey you,' Mark said, noticing her come in. 'I wondered when you'd be back. The boys waited up for you.'

'Mum!' Archie called, running out from the living room and hugging her. She pulled Mark into the embrace too, and gestured for a reluctant Josh to join them.

In that moment, she had everything she wanted. The horrors of the last few days were behind her for now, even though a number of them were going to need to be faced head on.

She'd sit Mark and the boys down and tell them what the consultant had said. Tomorrow. She'd have fallout to deal with at work, but that paled into insignificance in comparison to everything else. It could wait.

She kicked off her shoes and slumped down on the sofa in the living room, relieved beyond belief to put everything behind her for just a few hours.

'So,' Mark said, smiling. 'How was your day?'

IN COLD BLOOD

BOOK #3 IN THE RUTLAND CRIME SERIES

A body is found under Welland Viaduct on a bitterly cold winter morning. But this will be a murder investigation like no other.

As DI Caroline Hills and DS Dexter Antoine begin to unravel the dark secrets in the victim's life, they find themselves sucked into a web of lies and betrayal.

Rutland Police need to find the killer before it's too late. But with Caroline's health failing and their main witness suspiciously missing, the stakes couldn't be higher.

Dark histories, mysterious gifts and hidden secrets abound. But will they discover the truth before anyone else is killed in cold blood?

'Incredible' — BBC News

'A sensation' — The Guardian

Out now

ACKNOWLEDGMENTS

Although I'd always hoped *What Lies Beneath* would be received well, nothing could have prepared me for the reception it had — both in Rutland and beyond.

Within a week of the book being released, paperbacks had completely sold out twice over, with the book having sold more than ten times the anticipated launch sales. One bookshop chain had to be restocked at 10.30am on launch day, and eight separate print runs were needed just to get us through the first four weeks.

My agent had a busy time of it, too, fielding approaches from numerous television producers keen to snap up the series. At the time of writing, I can't offer any more on that, other than to say there are icebergs that move faster than the TV industry. If you could cross everything and pray to your personal flavour of god that we might see the series on TV sometime soon, that'd be lovely — cheers.

Although the best bits of *On Borrowed Time* are entirely down to me and I should rightly be given full credit and — in my honest opinion — a knighthood at the very least, I'm reliably informed I should find some people I can blame for the rubbish bits.

First of all, I need to thank my wife, Jo, because she's the one who can throw the fiercest punch. She's also quite handy to bounce plot ideas off, and she picks up on most of my embarrassing mistakes — on occasion, even in my books.

When I announced *What Lies Beneath*, I made the daft decision to offer signed copies to retailers in the Rutland area. That meant every single one of those books would have to pass through my hands for signing, and that we'd have to then organise getting them to the retailers ourselves, rather than relying on traditional distributors. To be fair, I thought we might only sell a few hundred. Whoops. So thank you, Jo, for organising and somehow maintaining an effective distribution chain. Thanks also to my mum and dad, who've been yanked out of retirement in order to turn their spare room into a warehouse and their small hatchback into a full-time delivery vehicle. It's hugely appreciated, and you're much cheaper than Parcelforce.

Enormous thanks to Caitlin White for all her help in hammering my loose ideas into a more workable form and doing a great job in helping me plan the book, before gently nudging my canoe down the First Draft River.

Mark Boutros did sod all on this one, so I'm not thanking him.

To Lucy, Beverley, Joanne, Helen and Manuela for your eagle eyes and ensuring this book isn't too much of an embarrassment — thank you.

The plot of *On Borrowed Time* needed some careful and

intricate research, and a large part of me wishes I'd never asked my good friend Simon Clarke to help me get the details of the train journey correct in chapter one. Simon quite rightly told me my plans weren't feasible and provided me with an extraordinary amount of incredibly useful information to back up his point. Naturally, I scoffed at this and said 'Sod it, I'll just say there were engineering works'.

Likewise, I need to thank the wonderful Kate Bendelow for her information on forensics. Kate is an extraordinarily talented woman and has been one of the country's top Crime Scene Investigators for over eighteen years. But even she wasn't immune to me being annoyed that little things like 'facts' and 'science' kept getting in the way of my story. At least, that's my defence if the police ever confiscate my phone and find the messages from Kate saying 'Any thoughts on how you're going to kill him before he's hanged?' and 'You could strangle him with a bag over his head'.

Enormous thanks also to Drs Vicki Barlow and Samantha Pickles, respectfully the Course Coordinator and Senior Lecturer in Forensic Science at the University of Bedfordshire, for their incredible help and information. From this fake University of Bedfordshire Doctor to two real, eminent and esteemed ones — thank you.

Thanks as always to Graham Bartlett, former ex-Chief Superintendent and City Commander of Brighton & Hove Police for all of his help and information. If it weren't for him, Caroline would be driving around in her Volvo with a stick-on siren (and I would've totally bought one for myself).

Thank you to PC Joe Lloyd for all his ongoing support. Keen readers may have noticed I rewarded him with a cameo in *On Borrowed Time*, which should keep him happy for a while.

Thanks also to Simon Cole QPM, Chief Constable of Leicestershire Police for all his ongoing support. Thank you especially for overlooking the bits where I had to completely ignore police procedure in favour of story!

It feels a bit strange to be thanking Agatha Christie, but I probably should. One or two of you may have noticed the occasional reference to Christie's *And Then There Were None*, not least in Owen Samuels's methods — and his name, which is a nod to her U. N. Owen. I had briefly flirted with the idea of calling him Owen Unwin, but thought that might have been a step too far in terms of smashing you into the clues face-first.

Thank you to Rosie Gurtovoy, Jonathan Sissons, Becky Wearmouth, Laura McNeil, Annabel Merullo and everyone else at PFD, my agents, who've been working hard to see my books translated abroad and adapted for television.

To Craig Thomson at W. F. Howes, for being such a pleasure to work with and so quick to get things moving on the audiobooks for the Rutland crime series. I'm really looking forward to working with you.

Thanks to everyone at BBC Radio Leicester, Rutland Radio (now scandalously gone, but which lives on in *On Borrowed Time*), the Rutland & Stamford Mercury (especially Maddy Baillie, who I forgot last time) and all of the other local media outlets for being so incredibly supportive. BBC East Midlands Today keep ignoring my emails, though, so I hope they find tiny and really annoying pieces of gravel in their shoes next time they put them on.

Thank you to all the local retailers in the Rutland area — and beyond — who've been so keen to stock the series. At the time of writing, that's Tim and the team at Walker's Books, Jonathan Young and everyone at the Rutland Water Visitor Centre, Debbie Oakes at Snapdragon, Karen Smith at Bourne Bookshop, Leanne Robbins at Budgens in Uppingham, Nicole-Marie Brown at Greetham Village Shop, Robin Carter at Hygge, Marcus Tyers at St Mary's Books in Stamford, Suraj from Whissendine Village Shop, Helen from Edith Weston Village Shop — plus Chris, Kristy and all the team at the Wisteria Hotel and all the folk at Collyweston Community Shop, Oh Curio in Harringworth, Ryhall Village Stores, South Witham Village Shop, and the Mill Street Wine Emporium in Oakham. I strongly suggest you pay them all a visit, but maybe not in the same day because that could get expensive.

To the wonderful book bloggers: Emily Ellis, Terry Sullivan, Gemma Myers, Yvonne Bastian, Nicki Murphy, Diane Hogg, Louise Cannon, Alyson Read, Joanna Larum, Sharon Rimmelzwaan, Linda Strong and Karen Cocking. Thank you.

To Xander and Jim for taking care of so many boring and menial tasks so I can focus on writing and getting drunk — thank you.

But most of all, thank you to my readers and the people of Rutland and beyond, who've been so incredibly supportive and positive about the series. It means the world to me that you've taken it to your hearts.

Shall we do it all again in a few months?

A SPECIAL THANK YOU TO MY PATRONS

Thank you to everyone who's a member of my Patreon program. Active supporters get a number of benefits, including the chance of having a character named after them in my books. In *On Borrowed Time*, PC Karina Gallagher and Nigel Gibbs were named after Patreon supporters.

With that, I'd like to give my biggest thanks to my small but growing group of readers who are currently signed up as Patreon supporters at the time of writing: Alexier (no surname given), Ann Sidey, Barbara Tallis, Carla Powell, Claire Evans, Darren Ashworth, Dawn Blythe, Dawn Godsall, Emiliana Anna Perrone, Emily Ellis, Estelle Golding, Geraldine Rue, Helen Weir, Jeanette Moss, Judy Hopkins, Julie Devonald Cornelius, Karina Gallagher, Leigh Hansen, Linda Anderson, Lisa Bayliss, Lisa Lewkowicz, Lisa-Marie Thompson, Liz Kentish, Lynne Davis, Lynne Lester-George, Mandy Davies, Maureen Hutchings, Nigel M Gibbs, Oriette Stubbs, Paul Wardle, Peter Tottman, ruralbob, Sally Catling, Sally-Anne Coton, Sim Croft (no relation), Sue (no surname), Sue

Martlew, Susan Fiddes, Sylvia Crampin, Tracey Clark, Tremayne Alflatt and Tyler Porter. You're all absolute superstars.

If you're interested in becoming a patron, please head over to patreon.com/adamcroft. Your support is enormously valuable.

HAVE YOU LISTENED TO THE RUTLAND AUDIOBOOKS?

The Rutland crime series is now available in audiobook format, narrated by Leicester-born **Andy Nyman** (Peaky Blinders, Unforgotten, Star Wars).

They are available from all good audiobook retailers and libraries now, published by W.F. Howes on their QUEST and Clipper imprints.

W.F. Howes are one of the world's largest audiobook publishers and have been based in Leicestershire since their inception.

W.F. HOWES LTD

ADAM CROFT

With over two million books sold to date, Adam Croft is one of the most successful independently published authors in the world, having sold books in over 120 different countries.

In February 2017, Amazon's overall Author Rankings briefly placed Adam as the most widely read author in the world at that moment in time, with J.K. Rowling in second place.

Adam is considered to be one of the world's leading experts on independent publishing and has been featured on BBC television, *BBC Radio 4*, *BBC Radio 5 Live*, the *BBC World Service*, *The Guardian*, *The Huffington Post*, *The Bookseller* and a number of other news and media outlets.

In March 2018, Adam was conferred as an Honorary Doctor of Arts, the highest academic qualification in the UK, by the University of Bedfordshire in recognition of his services to literature.

Adam presents the regular crime fiction podcast *Partners in Crime* with fellow bestselling author and television actor Robert Daws.